VULTURE'S WAKE

KIRSTY MURRAY

Holiday House / New York

Text copyright © Kirsty Murray 2009
First published in Australia in 2009 by Allen & Unwin.
83 Alexander St.
Crows Nest NSW 2065
Australia
First published in the United States of America by Holiday House in 2010.
All Rights Reserved
HOLIDAY HOUSE is registered in the U.S. Patent and Trademark Office.
Printed and bound in February 2010 at Maple Vail, York, PA, USA.
www.holidayhouse.com
First American Edition
1   3   5   7   9   10   8   6   4   2

Library of Congress Cataloging-in-Publication Data
Murray, Kirsty.
[Vulture's Gate]
Vulture's wake / by Kirsty Murray.—1st American ed.
p. cm.
Summary: In a future Australia, Callum and Bo, perhaps the only female survivor
of a bird virus, travel through a lawless, battle-ridden landscape as Callum seeks
his fathers and Bo tries to find a place to belong.
ISBN 978-0-8234-2282-1 (hardcover)
[1. Science fiction.   2. Survival—Fiction.   3. Women—Fiction.
4. Orphans—Fiction.   5. Australia—Fiction.]   I. Title.
PZ7.M9625Vu 2010
[Fic]—dc22
2009036020

Contents

1
The End

Callum felt the rumble of roadtrains, and froze. Black shadows skittered across the blinds as a convoy pulled up outside. Outstationers. If only he hadn't insisted on staying home alone. Instinctively, he dove for the floor.

The red neon sign at the gates of the compound flashed a warning across the surrounding desert, but Callum knew his fathers were still miles away.

Inside, the Elvis Presley cuckoo man jumped out of his clock and crooned the hour. Fighting down his fear, Callum crawled across the black-and-white tiled floor toward the kitchen, heading for the safety of the security apartment. Beneath him, the ground trembled. Above, the ceiling buckled and Callum covered his ears to block out the sound of Molotov cocktails exploding against the compound roof.

One by one, every alarm in the Refuge was triggered, screeching against the invasion.

As he pushed open the swing door to the kitchen, still keeping low to the floor, he heard the first crash. Someone was around the back trying to force the rear entrance. Metal grated against concrete. Any minute and they'd be through the second set of doors.

Callum combat-crawled on his belly across the floor as the rear wall exploded inward and pieces of debris hurtled through the kitchen. A cloud of dust and napalm-scented smoke billowed into the air. He glanced over his shoulder in time to see the grille of a roadtrain slam through the café's outer wall, sending shards of glass and steel across the pink vinyl booths. Callum bit his fist to stop himself from screaming. Then he saw the back doors collapse, and men charged across the wreckage, shouting and hooting amid the wail of alarms. He scrambled to his feet and made a dash for the security apartment entrance. He punched the keypad. Nothing happened. The system had shut down to prevent invasion. He was locked out.

Callum screamed, his throat raw with terror, as two men grabbed his arms and swung him into the air. They slammed his body against a wall and then reached for him again. Any moment now, they would smash his head against the ground and leave his broken body in the wreckage for Ruff and Rusty to find—a bloody signature.

Someone grabbed his ankle and dragged him outside, through the smoldering debris. The last thing Callum saw before he blacked out was the Elvis cuckoo clock falling into the rubble of Ruff & Rusty's Roadside Refuge.

2
Roboraptor Girl

Bo put two fingers between her teeth and gave a long, low whistle. The roboraptors were a faint shadow against the horizon, keeping low to the ground as they moved in for the kill.

Bo gave them enough time to finish off their prey and then whistled again to bring the raptor pack loping across the plain. As each one drew close, she touched it lightly on the skull and murmured its name—Chinky, Thumbelina, Cinderella, Silky. They bobbed their heads and ululated happily before scurrying into the underground bunker. Mr. Pinkwhistle was the last to return. He dropped a feral cat at her feet—a thin, stringy animal, but at least it was freshly killed. Anything was better than the salted desert rat she had been eating for the last few days.

She took the cat away from the burrow entrance and

squatted in the dirt to gut and skin it. The hot, fresh smell of its flesh made her mouth water. She threw the skin into the branches of a hakea tree to dry, then scraped a hole in the ground and buried the inedible parts of the cat.

By the time she crawled back down into the burrow, the roboraptors were in sleep mode, standing in a neat row against the rear wall of their den. Bo knelt in front of Mr. Pinkwhistle and rested her hand on his blunt snout. Before switching him off, she stroked his spine until he began to emit a low, purring sound. The other roboraptors whined faintly in response, acknowledging Mr. Pinkwhistle as the favored hunter. Satisfied, she reached under the jaw of each one in turn and switched them off. The afternoon sun would have charged them fully, and she wanted to make sure they stored the energy for tomorrow's dawn hunt.

Bo laid Poppy's recipe book on the kitchen table. Her grandfather's handwriting sloped across the paper like a horde of insects scurrying to the edge of the page. She smoothed the folio with one hand and twirled her meat cleaver in the other.

Bo's Cat Stew
   One cat, skinned and gutted. Remove hind legs and rub with oil or fat—feral pig lard is best. Put in pot.
   Add bush onions and pigweed. Scrape bitter seeds from handful of bush tomatoes and discard. Add bush tomato skins. Chuck in lump of rock salt. Seal pot tightly, push up through flue hole so sun beats

down on solar lid, and boil. You know it's cooking at the right temperature when you can hear a rolling, bubbling sound against the metal base.

Poppy had filled the margins of the book with little drawings and tips on where to find the best ingredients, how to thresh wild grasses, how to pickle desert fruits and salt meat to store for the lean times. Bo wished she had his voice stored as well as his words. With the roboraptors at rest and the stew cooking quietly in the solar flue, all she could hear was the thumping of her own heart.

When the meat was tender, Bo took a plate and sat in the entrance of the burrow, gazing out at the bleached desert. The stew tasted sweet, salty, and bitter all in the same mouthful. The sun sank lower toward the horizon. She shut her eyes and tried to imagine she was sitting next to Poppy and he was telling her what a good girl she was, what a fine cook, what a strong woman she would be one day. The westering sunlight felt hot against her face, and she pushed her hands against her eyes to stop them stinging. It was only when the sun dipped below the horizon and the cool desert night began to fall that she wedged a rock into the mouth of the burrow and went back underground.

3
Licorice Strapped

Callum felt sore all over. Even his tongue hurt. The metal torque around his neck chafed endlessly, and his ears were raw and bloodied where the Outstationers had cut out his microchips. But more unbearable than the physical pain was the emptiness he felt inside. After the violence of the kidnapping, he had expected worse to follow, but instead he had been left alone in the dark for days on end, only a sliver of light seeping into the back of the roadtrain as it rumbled across the desert.

There were two buckets in the truck, one for him to do his business in and one full of brackish drinking water. Once a day someone poked a crust of bread or a piece of salted meat through a slit in the door. No one spoke to him; no one checked on him.

All he could do was sit and wait and hope that the

Outstationers were holding him for ransom. Ruff and Rusty would pay to have him released. But deep inside, Callum suspected that the Outstationers had no interest in selling him back to his fathers. For months they had been conspiring to drive Ruff and Rusty away from the area, to rid the western desert of a last vital link to the Colony government. Without Ruff & Rusty's Refuge, there would be no safe house for Colony men trying to trade with the remnants of civilization in the west. Callum pressed his fists against his temples. He had to get back to his fathers.

The door was wrenched open and hot sunlight washed over him.

"Trading time, boy," said the Outstationer, unshackling Callum's chain from the wall and dragging him out onto the road. Callum stumbled along in the man's wake, the soles of his bare feet scorched by the burning ground.

A man in a shiny leather vest and dusty black leather trousers stood waiting. Flanking him was a ragtag group of desert wanderers whose clothes were stained with red dust. The leather-clad man stared at Callum from beneath bushy eyebrows.

"He's a good 'un, Floss. You won't be sorry," said the Outstationer, pushing Callum forward. "Been raised by a pair of proper fathers. He's a real boy. Speaks nice. Keeps his nose clean. Guaranteed. This sort are worth training. You know I wouldn't sell you a dud. Pig-boys only last until they're fifteen but you'll get years out of this one."

Floss opened Callum's mouth and looked inside. He parted Callum's hair and checked his scalp, looked into his eyes, and then twisted his arms behind his back.

"Ouch!" said Callum.

"Bit of a precious petal, isn't he?"

"Nah, he's got enough grit. Cries a little, but that's what you expect from the fathered ones. That's what makes 'em worth having."

Floss pushed back Callum's head, drew one finger along his jaw, and smiled. Callum wanted to bite him.

Floss handed a bag of a sticky black substance to the Outstationer and took hold of Callum's chain. He led him through a ghetto of battered roadtrains and trailers to where a clutter of cages was assembled. Then he pushed him into a long, narrow enclosure on wheels and shackled his chain to the bars. Callum sank to his knees and smashed his chain against the metal floor in despair. The sound drew a cry of alarm from the occupants of the other cages. Most of the animals in the freak show looked like a cross between frogs and cats. Their back legs were smooth and amphibious but their forelegs were thick with fur. When Callum was small, he'd secretly longed to have a chimera as a pet, even though his fathers had told him they were illegal freaks. And now he was part of the freak show, too. It made him feel queasy. If this outfit was trading in chimeras and boys, they were the lowest type of criminals.

"Oi, dreamboy," said Floss, returning. He pushed the handle of a bullwhip into the cage and poked Callum in the ribs. "Get out of those rags and put this on." He threw a handful of clothes through the bars.

Despite his misery, Callum was glad to take off his old shirt and jeans that were caked in dirt and blood. The new outfit was a pair of silky, black leatherlike pants and a black vest. He tried to rake his hand through his hair but it was so stiff with dust that it stood straight up in matted clumps.

The cage was too small to stand in so Callum had to lie flat and wriggle into the close-fitting costume. With his eyes fixed on the roof of the cage, he could ignore the fact that Floss was watching him. When he was dressed, Floss opened the cage and tugged on his chain. "C'mon. Training time."

Inside a silver and purple tent, three motorcycles were circling the "cage of death" and another was looping giddily inside the rim of a giant wheel. The tent reverberated with the roar of engines. Callum groaned. Of all the businesses to wind up with, he had been sold into the meanest motorcycle outfit in the western desert. Ruff and Rusty had told him about the nomad performers that drifted from outstation to mining camp, causing trouble wherever they went, trading in drugs and children and remnant technologies. Despite their dark reputation, they could always find an audience. The Colony wanted to stamp them out but they never stayed in one place long enough for the Colony's Squadrones to catch them.

Floss suddenly jerked the chain, hard.

"Leave off," Callum snapped, holding the torque to stop it biting into his skin. "You're hurting me."

"Oooh, a cranky dog," said Floss, laughing. "Okay, poodle-boy, time for you to jump through a few hoops."

Floss undid the chain and dragged Callum by the wrist to where another bearded giant sat astride an old Harley-Davidson motorcycle. The two men could have been twins.

"Here's our new pup," said Floss.

The other biker looked at Callum appraisingly, then suddenly grabbed the front of his vest and lifted him off the ground. For a moment, Callum stared into his scarred face. Then the man threw him across to Floss, who caught him with one hand. "Nice weight, see?" said Floss. "Easy to toss around."

"Okay, kid," barked the biker. "Can you do a somersault?"

"A what?"

"Throw yourself in the dirt and roll, boy."

Callum shrugged his shoulders and looked at the ground.

"Christ, Floss, I told you we wanted one that could bend."

Floss seized Callum by one ankle, held him upside down, then shook him. Hard. Callum had to pull himself up like a possum and grab his feet so that his teeth didn't rattle.

"See, Dental, he's got good reflexes. He'll train up quick." Floss threw Callum down in the sawdust, knocking the wind out of him. The pain in his ribs made him gasp. Then Floss pulled out an electric cattle prod. "What do you want him to do now?"

Callum lay in the sawdust, curled into a ball. He would not give them the satisfaction of seeing him cry. But when Floss poked him with the cattle prod, a surge of electricity made him kick out in pain.

"Get up," said Floss. "Tell us your handle, boy."

"My what?"

"Your name, or don't they give names to you cybrid jam-jars anymore?"

"I'm not a cybrid. I have two fathers."

"So what did they call you?"

"My name is Callum."

The men rolled their eyes toward each other and snorted with amusement.

"We'll call you Dog. You'll need a name that bites, not a fancy-schmancy baby name. We're a two-man show. Two men and a dog, that is. Youse our dog from now on."

"What's that meant to mean?"

"You chase after the bikes," said Dental. "We've got a few tricks we're gonna teach you. First, we check your balance. You got no balance, we'll sell you to the next Outstationer looking for dog meat." He put out his wide, square hand. "Step up."

Callum gritted his teeth as he put one foot on Dental's palm. He wobbled crazily as the big man hoisted him into the air.

"Steady up and step across to Floss's hand."

For the next half hour Callum practiced stepping back and forth between them. Then they made him stand on their shoulders while they held his ankles. Sweat trickled down his neck as he struggled to stay centered. By the end of the afternoon, he could stand without them holding him at all.

Dental lowered him to the ground and reached into his pocket. He pulled out a handful of tiny biscuits and threw them onto the ground in front of Callum.

"You done well. Like I said, this gig is about balance.

Once you can balance, then you learn how to bend. Like a licorice strap. The last bonehead wouldn't bend, wouldn't train up proper. We snapped him in two. If you bend, you won't break."

Callum stared at the biscuits lying in the sawdust and knew, despite his humiliation, that he would eat them. As Floss came toward him with the chain, he also knew that he would learn to bend, he would learn to survive. He would never let them break him.

4
Shooting Nightbirds

Bo touched her gun and felt the coolness of it. She didn't want to go out tonight but Poppy had taught her routines that were important. She took down her catskin shawl from the hook and slung it around her shoulders.

Outside, the sky was awhirl with stars. Nightbirds soared above the sleeping desert, circling for prey. Bo spread the catskin on the ground and lay down. She looked through the viewfinder and rested her finger on the trigger. When the first wedge of black wing came into view, a dark shadow against the stars, she narrowed her gaze and fired. The nightbird plummeted to earth, landing with a dull *thwack* on the rocky desert plain. More black silhouettes flitted against the starry sky, trying to escape her bullets, but they were easy targets.

She had the fifth nightbird in her finder when

something caught her eye. Far away, on the edge of the horizon, a light flickered and then died. Outstationers. Bo's skin prickled with unease. She remembered Poppy saying the landmines would keep the two of them safe, as long as they stayed inside their territory. But Poppy had been wrong. She pushed away the memory of his face on the night they discovered how vulnerable they were.

As if to echo her thoughts, one of the mines blew. She felt it through the ground and heard the roar of the explosion roll across the stony desert. Someone was trying to cross the boundary of her hunting grounds.

One step at a time, sweeping away her tracks, she backed into the opal cave. A telltale sliver of light seeped out under the doorway and she hurried to switch off every lumina in the burrow.

Now she knew why she hadn't wanted to go outside. A part of her had sensed trouble was near. Sometimes she knew things before they happened. A change in the weather days before it came across the desert. Where water lay, as if her skin picked up the scent of it. Even if she couldn't name the thing, she felt its impending arrival.

"Woman's 'twition," Poppy had said. "'Twition ain't rational." He didn't believe in it, but the night he was murdered Bo had sensed they were both in danger and she had been right. She knew she should always respect her instincts. Right now, her "'twition" was telling her to go deep, to get away from the surface where some form of sensor might pick up the warmth of her skin and bury every sign of life in the deepest ground. She pointed the beam from her laser through a small window that overlooked the Wombator's den. If she set him to work tonight, he would have a new, deeper burrow carved out for her by morning—but would his vibrations alert the Outstationers to her presence?

She lay on her belly and then wriggled through a portal into the lowest room of the burrow, pulling a rock in place to jam the entrance. Against the back wall, her roboraptors were stationed in standby mode. She spread the catskin shawl on the ground and settled herself beneath the roboraptors, their bowed heads above her. It felt safer being here with Mr. Pinkwhistle so close. She wrapped one hand around his foreleg, just to remind herself of the strength in the beast-machine.

She tried not to think about the night the Outstationers killed Poppy. Remembering was like opening a wound, as if all the blood was running out of her onto the desert stones. The hunting grounds had grown barren, but Poppy wouldn't hunt outside them. He thought they were safe inside the ring of landmines. Then that night, when they were on the very edge of their territory, the Outstationers crossed the boundary. What was the last thing Poppy had said before the murderers were upon them? "Scuttle."

"Scuttle," she whispered to herself. Poppy had taught her how to scuttle—how to disappear from view, how to move between rocks and hard places like water, like the silveriest skink. Bo knew how to scuttle. But she didn't know how to stop the cavernous hurt opening up in her chest at the thought of Poppy. There was only one thing that would push it away.

"*Once upon a time in a faraway kingdom . . .*" she whispered into the blackness. She wanted to hear the susurration of the words, like a prayer, like an ancient telling that would make her feel safe. The words hung in the air of the opal cave. A moment later, another landmine exploded.

5
Gambling with Fate

Callum ran one finger over the line of notches in the corner of his cage. Three months. Every single day that he had worked for Floss and Dental was marked by a tiny notch made with his front teeth. Now there were ninety-two toothy indentations.

Callum had grown lean and wiry since his capture but he still hadn't grown accustomed to the confines of his cage. As much as he hated being made to bend and spin in the circus ring, it was better than the long hours trapped in the freak show.

They'd been driving all day, criss-crossing the red brown desert, searching for the next cluster of outstations. The trucks rolled through silent country while Callum lay in his cage, bathed in sweat. Finally they came to a stop on a gibber plain. Tango, the striped tiger-monkey, picked at his fleas and snarled at the small dust devils that swirled past their encampment. The chimeras shifted restlessly, making weird mewling sounds that sent shivers up Callum's spine.

As darkness fell, the chimeras began to pace in their enclosures. Tango rattled the bars of his cage. They were desperate to stretch their limbs in the ring, but there would be no show tonight. The desert lay still and empty on every side of the encampment.

Callum drew a deep breath and stretched his arms through the bars. If he could only find some way to forget how uncomfortable he was, a night alone could almost be a treat. He was tired of being thrown between Dental and Floss, flipped and tossed through the air from one speeding motorcycle to the other while an audience of drunken Outstationers hooted and roared, hoping to see him fall. He began to hum quietly—a ballad about sunshine, rain, and wide blue skies—shutting his eyes against his prison and the company of the agitated chimeras. In his mind's eye he could see Rusty sitting on the end of a bed with his guitar and Ruff in the doorway, nodding his head in time to the music and then joining in, his deep voice adding a rich harmony. Fighting down his emotions, he began to sing the song, trying to hold the vision of his fathers. His voice rang out across the rocky desert.

For a moment, he opened his eyes and looked out through the bars of his cage. The chimeras had fallen silent. Tango's yellow eyes flashed, and the monkey stretched out his arms, palms turned up to the sky. Callum understood. When he came to the end of the song, he started another and the chimeras sat quietly, their restless misery stilled by the music.

It was only when he got to the end of his last song that he saw Dental's beady black eyes staring at him from across the compound. Callum turned away and curled into a ball in the far corner of his cage. He had given too much away. He had let Dental see into his heart. Nothing good would come of it.

The next morning, Dental opened the cage, undid Callum's chain, and whistled. "Hup, ya bloody mongrel." He knew it annoyed Callum but it was the same taunt every morning.

As he was led into the Big Top to practice, he muttered his own name over and over. No one called him Callum anymore. "Dog," "Mutt," "Mongrel" was all they ever shouted at him. He was afraid that if he didn't repeat his true name to himself, he would forget who he used to be and become the thing they called him.

Dental whistled the tune that Callum had sung the night before and yanked Callum's chain. "C'mon, howler," he sneered. "Sing us a tune." Suddenly he yanked the chain so hard that Callum was forced to the ground.

Callum tried to stifle a whimper of pain. He knew that Dental took sadistic pleasure in watching him gasp for breath.

"How many times have I told you not to treat the kid like that?" shouted Floss, snatching the chain from Dental. He unshackled Callum and checked the marks on his neck.

"We can't afford to replace him. You break his neck like you did the last one and I swear I'll have your kneecaps."

"You will, will you?" sneered Dental, puffing his chest out like an angry rooster.

Floss pushed Callum to one side and turned on Dental. "Listen, I bought him with my stash. You pay me, and you can do what you like to him."

While they argued, Callum slipped through the flaps of the tent, and ran out into the wide, empty desert. There was nowhere to hide on the flat plains but he ran anyway, leaping over the pebbly ground, kicking up flurries of red dust, running full tilt into the harsh morning sunlight.

He hadn't gone far when he heard shouting and the roar of the bikes approaching. But he didn't stop running. He dove to one side as grit and dirt flew into his face. The sheer act of defiance made him feel alive even as the bikers circled him in a wide arc, letting him run himself ragged. They might punish him, but he knew they wouldn't mow him down. If they did, they'd have to buy another dog-boy.

Wet with sweat and breathless with exhaustion, Callum fell to his knees. He covered his face with his hands and waited for the moment when one of the men would reach out and drag him back to the Big Top. He prayed it would be Floss but it was Dental's heavy hand that fell upon his neck. With one swift movement Dental wrenched Callum from the ground and onto the tank of his bike. Then he leaned forward and a spray of spittle covered Callum's neck as he hissed, "Floss plays the big man but never forget I'm top dog around here."

Callum shrank away from Dental, clinging to the

motorcycle's tank. He knew that if Dental wanted to have his way, no one could stop him, not even Floss.

Callum woke with a start as a hand groped his leg. He scrambled to a corner of the cage. In the darkness he couldn't make out who his attacker was. All the circus lights were out, the canvas of the tents flapping lazily in the night breeze.

"We got business, you and me," said Dental, shining a flashlight into Callum's face and flashing his jagged teeth in a sharklike smile.

He dragged Callum by his torque to one of the long, shining trucks that carried the motorbikes. He pushed a button and the side of the truck unfolded. Moonlight washed over the pearly white tank and silver spokes of the biggest bike Callum had ever seen. Embossed on the center of the tank was a blue heart edged with gold.

"Beautiful, isn't she?" said Dental, wheeling her down the ramp.

Callum nodded. He knew it had to be a rare machine. None of the other bikes was called "she."

"We don't use the Daisy-May much. Too precious. She gets hurt and no one's got the art to fix her no more. But she is one beautiful getaway machine." Dental ran his hand over the tank and smiled as he swung his leg over her. "Get on, woofer."

Callum shifted from foot to foot. "Where's Floss?" he asked. "Why isn't he coming, too?"

With one quick jerk, Dental yanked Callum into the air and then threw him down like a rag doll onto the front of the bike. He leaned forward, his long arms trapping Callum between the tank and his body.

"Where are you taking me?"

"To round up sheep, Dog."

Dental kick-started the engine, and the Daisy-May started with a soft whirr. Callum gripped the seat with his knees. As the bike picked up speed, he lay down across the tank, hanging on to the warm, smooth metal with both hands. They were traveling fast, skimming over the stony ground. The wind felt like needles against Callum's bare skin. Dental hit a button and a transparent blue hood rose up from the front of the bike and settled over them so they were enclosed inside a bubble.

The desert whipped past. Callum remembered peyote bikes like the Daisy-May roaring along the highway outside the Refuge, and Rusty whistling and saying, "He's doing a Doppler!" Maybe that strange tension in the air meant they were approaching the speed of sound. Dental leaned down hard, pressing against Callum. The speedometer nudged 750 miles per hour.

Beneath the blue hood, the air was rank with Dental's body odor. When Dental stopped the Daisy-May at the gates of a silvery gray outstation and raised the hood, Callum gulped down the sharp night air.

Two guards stepped forward to run a weapons detector over both Dental and Callum and then waved the Daisy-May through the gates. They rode slowly until they came to an open square where hundreds of men sat around in groups, gambling at long tables. The air was thick with smoke from hookahs, pipes, and cigarettes.

"Does Floss know we're here?" asked Callum. It felt safer to bait Dental when there were other men around.

"Will you shut up about Floss!"

"You guys, you're sworn brothers, aren't you? Won't he worry about where we've gone?" he asked, watching as Dental's face contorted with rage.

The big man lunged forward and sank his jagged teeth into the top of Callum's ear. Callum squealed with pain. Then Dental lifted him up so they were face-to-face.

"Listen, poodle-boy. I'm not one of your dads. I don't do sworn brotherhood. That's for Colony mugs like your old men. I'm not out to save the bleeding civilization. I'm out for me, Dental. Got it?"

Holding his bloody ear, Callum nodded. Dental found a seat at the end of a bench and pulled Callum onto his knee, securing him firmly in place with one hand as he gathered up his playing chips. On the table were ingots of gold, silver, and platinum, small clear bags full of pills and sticky substances, and small boxes of remnant technologies—microchips and computer hardware. Callum couldn't follow the rules of the game but there were a lot of small white squares with black markings moving around the table. As the night wore on, little beads of sweat began to gather on Dental's brow and drip down into his beard. He kept smiling his sharklike grin but it was clear he was losing. Callum felt a small rush of pleasure.

Late in the night, one of the gamblers pushed a bulging green leather wallet into the center of the table.

"You can't cover a bet like that, can you? I reckon you're out of this round, stranger."

The other gamblers began pushing forward bags of pills and ingots of metal. The dealer checked each bid carefully before accepting them.

"I'm not out yet," said Dental. He reached into his jacket, pulled out a clear bag filled with a sticky black substance, and tossed it at the dealer.

For a long, silent moment the wizened man sniffed the contents. Then he threw Dental's stake back to him, shaking his head. "Too piss poor."

"Not so fast. I got a sweetener here that'll round the bid." He grabbed Callum by his torque and lifted him onto the table. "Heard you say how you like howlers around here. Heard your last one met with an accident. This one's a treat. He can bend, too. Put him to any use you want. He's worth a lot to me. Good little performer. Take him as my stake."

"He's a bleedin' runt," scoffed one of the men.

"No, he's a little beauty. Still got his baby-boy voice—sweet like." Dental shoved Callum into the center of the table. "Go on, Dog, howl," he commanded.

Callum looked into the faces of the Outstationers and felt his throat constrict. For an instant, he thought of doing as he was told. But he had a creeping feeling that life would be even worse at this outstation than at the circus. He stayed mute.

"Sing, you pig-child," said Dental, jumping up onto the bench and shaking Callum by his neck. Suddenly, in a flash of inspiration, Callum knew exactly what he should do. It was a trick that had always scared his fathers. He contracted his stomach muscles and forced himself to belch so loudly that saliva and vomit filled his mouth. Then he let it drool over his lips. At the same time he furrowed his brow and rolled his eyes back in his head until he knew only the whites were showing.

By the time Callum had finished the trick, the gamblers were backing away from him, as if he were diseased.

"Damn you," said Dental. Quick as a ferret, he pulled a small blowpipe out from behind his ear and shot three darts, one into the face of each of the nearest gamblers. As panic ensued, Dental swept all the bids from the table into the folds of his black leather jacket. Grabbing Callum with his free hand and kicking chairs and benches from their path, he jumped back onto the Daisy-May. He slammed Callum down on the tank, shoved the stolen winnings into a saddlebag, and gunned the accelerator.

Men were shouting and sirens wailing as the Daisy-May tore through the streets of the outstation, ploughing past the guards at the gates. They opened fire as the Daisy-May shot out into the desert. The bike shuddered and lost speed. Callum turned to see Dental's face contorted in pain as he fumbled for the switch that would bring the protective blue hood over them.

Callum knew this was his moment. All the months of learning to bend, of making his muscles stretch and flex in the ring, could finally serve him. Before he could feel afraid, he turned onto his back and lay flat against the tank, his legs curled against his chest. Grasping the handlebars of the motorcycle with both hands, he employed a version of a stunt where he would put his feet against Floss's chest and then spring into a handstand. Now he put both feet squarely against Dental's chest and kicked out with all his strength. The Daisy-May careered to one side. Quickly, Callum struck again, this time bringing his heels sharply into Dental's chin. He saw a little spurt of blood as Dental's lip was pierced by his own front tooth. Then Dental was gone and the bike was fishtailing along the desert road with Callum hanging on wildly.

The sirens of the outstation grew louder as Callum flipped himself over. He could hear the roar of vehicles in pursuit. He gripped the handlebars tightly with both hands and let the throttle out. As the bike picked up speed, he lowered his body until he was lying flat along the seat, until he felt he was melding to the machine. To the west lay the circus, to the east, the Outstationers. He gunned the accelerator and turned the Daisy-May southward.

6
Lost and Found

Bo watched a silvery gray dawn creep over the eastern horizon. Keeping the roboraptors clear of the minefield, she paced the boundary until she came across the exploded landmine. The remains of an Outstationer and his broken vehicle lay scattered across the ground. She hung her head in a moment of silent respect, as Poppy had taught her. Then she scraped a shallow grave for his remains and set about laying a replacement mine farther afield, marking out the distances between the old mines and the new, ensuring that nothing could cross the boundaries of Tjukurpa Piti without warning.

When she had finished, she looked back toward the hunting ground and sighed. She had taken every precaution before setting out in the dawn light. She had checked the sensors for any signs of human activity and set the

Wombator to work, programming it to dig another layer of tunnels beneath the upper burrow with emergency escape routes fanning out in two new directions. She knew she should turn back and hunt within the boundary of mines but the thought of bagging only another stringy feral cat made her heart sink. There were no trees left inside her hunting ground, no desert fruits or roots to forage. Even though she knew Poppy would have disapproved, she herded the roboraptors through the minefield and into the wider desert. The morning was still and cool. It was the best time for hunting. The roboraptors were excited by the rising sun and gamboled along at her ankles making low purring sounds. The desert was her own.

She whistled two short commands and the roboraptors scurried ahead, fanning out into the low scrub, sending up little spurts of red earth from beneath their clawed feet. She hitched her string bag higher on her shoulder and picked up speed. She would have to walk for miles before she reached the old creekbed. It had been dry for decades, but Bo knew that along its banks were the best places for digging out soft roots. An artesian well buried deep in the soil fed the long, stringy vegetables that she loved. She clipped some handfuls of graybeard grass and lined the string bag with it. It would be useful later for straining the sludgy black water that pooled in crevices along the creekbed. As she descended the rise above the creek, she pulled up a naked woollybutt tussock and added it to the string bag. It was small and dried out, but there was still enough seed on the long stems to make it worth taking home.

Reaching the dry creekbed at last, she squatted down on its banks and began to dig at the base of a withered tree. It took her twenty minutes to reach the root network that housed dead grubs, and she was cross and sweaty by the time she found a finger-thick root and hacked it out. Her pleasure turned to disappointment when she peeled off the outer layer and found the grubs inside had turned powdery. She licked her fingers and dipped them into the chalky remains. At least the grub-dust was still sweet and nutty tasting.

She sat back on her heels and listened for the sound of the roboraptors. The last time they had ventured outside the hunting grounds, Mr. Pinkwhistle had come back with a human hand in his jaws. Bo had scraped a hole in the nearest sandy patch of desert and buried it deep so the raptors wouldn't find it again. No matter how hungry she was, there were some taboos she would never break.

Bo noticed a flurry of dust on the rise above the opposite bank and the tips of the roboraptors' tails, erect and quivering. It seemed an odd place to catch something. Only a very stupid or sick animal would be caught on high ground where it was in clear view of approaching predators. Usually the roboraptors cornered their prey in outcrops of rock or chased them to ground on the flat plains.

Bo heard an unearthly cry. Seconds later, a boy stumbled over the crest of the rise and rolled down the sandy bank of the creek. Bo cried out in surprise. The roboraptors let out a group ululation of triumph and sped down the embankment to where the boy now lay motionless in the dry creekbed. Bo jumped to her feet and ran. By the time she got there, Mr. Pinkwhistle was standing on the boy's head while the rest of the raptor pack perched on other parts of him, sending out the whine that signaled for Bo to help them carry home heavy prey.

Bo swatted the roboraptors away and knelt down. The boy was scrawny and his black hair stood up in ratty spikes. Bruises mottled his bare arms and the backs of his legs where his trousers were torn. He was out cold. Bo rolled him over and he flopped onto his back. The roboraptors danced on the spot with excitement.

"Dumb," she said irritably, tapping each one between the eyes so they knew they had made a mistake. "Bad food."

She leaned in close to the boy's body and sniffed his skin. He smelt of sweat and dust, something sweet and something sour. Resting her head against his chest, she listened to the sound of his heartbeat, felt the gentle rise and fall of his breath. She was relieved he was still alive.

The sky began to turn a smoky orange. Soon the morning cool would give way to scorching heat. If she left the boy unconscious in the dry creekbed, he'd be dead by midday. Maybe that would be a good thing. Then again, if he was an Outstationer's boy they might come looking for him, and if they found him before he died he would tell them about the herd of roboraptors. They would suspect that a techno-hunter was nearby, that Poppy hadn't been solo. She'd never be able to venture out of the hunting grounds again.

Taking her sharpest blade, she cut a section of bark big enough for a sled from a nearby tree. Using a coil of wire that was attached to her belt, she fashioned a series of harnesses for the roboraptors. She hauled the boy onto her shoulder, then laid him on the bark and snapped her fingers at Mr. Pinkwhistle. As the roboraptors dragged the makeshift bark sled and its cargo up the embankment and back to Tjukurpa Piti, Bo swept their tracks with a bundle of twigs, scattering rocks in their wake to hide the trail.

When they had navigated their way across the minefield, Bo carried the boy, like a sack of bones, into the burrow. She took him down to a dark cave beyond the kitchen and laid him on a pile of rugs. He made a murmuring noise and curled into a ball, like a dead bush rat.

For a while, Bo squatted beside him, studying his sleeping face. It had been so long since she'd seen a living human being up close that every aspect of his features fascinated her. His eyes were set wide apart and framed by high, arching brows. His long black eyelashes lay like butterfly wings against his cheeks. She traced her finger along his cheekbone. His skin was smooth and silky. His lips were dark pink and he had a small dimple in his chin. He was like a boy out of a fairy story. Before leaving him, she gently rested her cheek against his, savoring his sleepy warmth.

It was almost night when Bo heard the boy screaming. She slid down the connecting passage from the main living area. The sounds of his cries bounced off the stone and opal and echoed through the tunnel.

"Shush!" she said, as she held up a lumina and light filled the cave. Still the boy screamed, eyes scrunched up, mouth open wide.

Bo stared at him, perplexed. She'd forgotten how people talked to each other. It was easy with the raptors. One word was enough. She frowned and tried again. "Shush!"

The boy opened his eyes long enough to actually see her and he caught his breath. For a split second, he fell silent. Bo reached out a hand to him in a gesture of friendship and he started up again. His screams made her head hurt. She tried to remember what Poppy had done when she was very small and upset.

Gently but firmly, she grabbed the boy by both shoulders and leaned in close to him. He was so surprised he didn't struggle. Drawing a deep breath, she blew a soft stream of air onto the side of his neck. He tried to pull away but she drew him closer, wrapping her arms around him so he was pinned against her body. She cradled his head in one hand and blew a puff of air onto each of his scrunched-up eyelids. Startled, he stopped screaming and began to sob instead, his body growing limp in her arms. Bo continued to blow little puffs of air onto different parts of his face. His expression grew very still, as if he were frozen. He opened his dark eyes and looked at her just as she was blowing a long, steady stream of breath onto his forehead.

"I'm not dead, am I?" he asked.

"Dead?" she echoed.

"Maybe you're some spook from the underworld? But I didn't think hell would be like this."

Bo suddenly felt aware of his body pressed against her

own and the vibrations of his voice in her chest. She let go of him and backed away.

The boy shuddered and looked about him for the first time.

"What is this place? Where am I? How did I get here? Who are you? Why did you do that to me?"

Bo knew she was meant to form whole sentences in answer to his questions but it had been too long. There were too many "who," "what," "where," "how," and "whys." She had to concentrate to retrieve the words from the back of her brain.

"Tjukurpa Piti."

"You don't speak English," he said, disappointed.

"I speak. I understand," she replied. She could feel sounds bubbling up from somewhere deep inside her, her own words, not storybook ones. She could feel her mouth struggling to form her thoughts into sounds, feel the warmth of them against her throat. It wasn't like storytelling. She had to make words from nowhere.

"Me Callum," said the boy, pointing to himself. "You? . . ."

Bo rolled her eyes. The pretty boy was smiling at her as if she were a simpleton.

"I am Boadicea," she said, trying to make the words sound sharp and resonant. "I found you."

"Are you one of those ferals, then?" he asked, leaning in closer and studying her as if she were a curiosity. "You don't look like an Outstationer, so what are you? Cybrid? Hybrid? Where did you come from?"

The questions ricocheted around the small chamber like bullets. Bo's head began to ache. She picked up the lumina and started down the tunnel, crawling quickly back to the main room.

"Hey!" called Callum, as he dropped down onto his belly and started to wriggle along behind her. "Hey, Booditchy, wait up. Don't leave me. Don't leave me in the dark."

But Bo simply moved faster, wishing fervently that she had never brought the boy home.

7
Tjukurpa Piti

Bo could hear Callum gasping behind her as he scrabbled to catch up. When she reached the brightly lit living area she felt a fleeting desire to seal the boy in the lower tunnels forever, but instead she waited for him, drumming her fingers on the kitchen table. He whimpered as he crawled out of the tunnel and stood upright. Bo followed his gaze as he stared at his surroundings in surprise. The cave was different now that it sheltered a stranger. The bulbous stone oven looked ungainly and the small kitchen and dining area seemed cluttered with wooden bowls and storage jars. Piles of salvaged old-tech machinery reached to the ceiling, almost obscuring the rough, stippled walls.

"Crazy," said the boy. He took a step toward the weathered old couch but his body began to crumple before he reached it. He steadied himself against a wall and turned back to stare at Bo. "This place is bizarre. You live here?"

Bo shrugged and turned away from him, as though he would magically disappear if she ignored him. She gathered up her long, silky brown hair and knotted it into a chignon before setting about tidying the kitchen. There was no reason to clean it, but Callum's presence made her see everything in a different light. She knew he was watching her and she pulled the ties of her shirt tighter, as if by fastening her clothes she could shut him out.

"What's this stuff?" he asked, scratching at a jagged piece of sparkling silver gray stone embedded in the wall.

"Opal."

"Isn't that bad luck or something?"

Bo ignored him and began straightening the shelves.

"So it was you who saved me from those beastie things?" he said after a long silence.

Bo could hear the shift in his tone. It was warmer, as if he might even admire her for helping him. Suddenly the full meaning of what he'd said sank in. "Beastie things?" she said.

"Those giant rats." He frowned and put one hand to his forehead. "It was you that saved me when they came to eat me, wasn't it?"

Bo laughed and then gave a low whistle. It was answered by a cry from deep underground and the sound of the approaching roboraptors scurrying from the lower depths, spiraling up toward them. Callum's face grew white. He lunged at the kitchen table, sweeping containers onto the floor as he scrambled to climb on top of it.

As the roboraptors swarmed into the cave, he picked up a wooden bowl to fling at them. Bo snatched it from his grasp.

"No! These are children. Roboraptors. My children."

Callum's face crumpled in disgust. "You can't mean children. They're not even pets. They're machines."

Bo scooped Mr. Pinkwhistle into her arms, holding him close with one hand and stroking the underside of his jaw. "My finest hunter." She frowned. She wanted her speech to flow but it was jammed somewhere in the back of her head, a whirling mass of complex sentences and lost words. She took a deep breath and they began to tumble out of her in a rush. "Poppy and I salv—salvaged, built, repaired, made new. We soldered, wired all from wreckage, debris, rubbish, broken, twisted remnants." She sighed and thought carefully before she crafted her next sentence. "We made them whole again."

"What are you?" said Callum. "Are you a chimera? Is there someone who owns you? What are you doing out here all by yourself?"

Bo blushed and carefully put Mr. Pinkwhistle down on the floor. "What are *you*?" she said sharply.

"You can't answer questions with questions."

Bo shut her green eyes and stood still for a long moment, dredging from distant memory.

"Once upon a time, I was very small. Poppy brought me here. I grew up here. I belong here," said Bo, slowly enunciating each word. "You . . . fell from the sky."

Callum laughed bitterly. "I wish."

All the nervous energy drained out of him and he

slumped onto his knees, as if every bone in his body were aching. He lay down on the table, flat on his back, and stared at the ceiling. "I ran away on the Daisy-May." He laughed at the accidental rhyme even as he winced, folding his arms tightly across his body. With his eyes shut he looked small and vulnerable again. He lay without speaking, his face etched with pain. Bo quietly herded the roboraptors into their den.

"Come," she said touching Callum gently on the shoulder. He flinched momentarily but then meekly let her lead him across the cave to the long sofa. When she wrapped a fur rug around his shoulders, he didn't resist. "The Daisy-May," he muttered. "I should go and find her. I have to find her before they do. I have to keep moving."

"Not now," said Bo, pulling the rug up to cover him, tucking him in as if he were a tiny child.

Callum looked drowsily up at the high shelves that lined the walls of the burrow.

"What are they?" he asked, pointing.

"Books."

Bo pulled a red volume from the shelf and handed it to him.

"How do you turn them on?" he asked.

Bo laughed. "They are for reading, not for turning on."

Bo took the book back and began to read aloud. *"Once upon a time a king and a queen lived peacefully with their twelve children, who were all boys. One day the king said to his wife, 'If the thirteenth child you are about to bear turns out to be a girl, then the twelve boys will have to be put to death . . .'"* At first she read haltingly but then the words began to flow, weaving a cat's cradle of sounds that lulled the boy into a deep and dreamless sleep.

The sun hung low, a hazy orb in the western skies. Bo watched the boy squinting uneasily into the light. He had slept through the morning and woken early in the afternoon, insistent that he had to find his vehicle before someone else did.

"Mines. Step carefully," said Bo, snatching Callum's wrist and forcing him to follow in her footsteps. When they had reached clear ground, Bo tapped Mr. Pinkwhistle three times on the base of his spine. He lowered his head and emitted a whirring noise in the back of his throat before scurrying out into the desert, sending little puffs of dust into the air.

Bo set out after the raptor at a run. Soon she heard Callum calling after her.

"Boo, Boy, Bo, whatever you call yourself, slow down! We must be close by now," he said, as he struggled to keep pace.

Bo touched the tracks of the raptor. "No. Still far away."

"How did you get me back to your place if it's so far?"

She turned to Callum and smiled. "My children helped."

The boy grimaced, and Bo wanted to shake him. Should she not call them her children? Was there something wrong with that? She had spent half the morning in the roboraptors' den, practicing her sentences on them so that she could speak properly to this boy, and still she couldn't seem to make their conversations work, couldn't make him understand what she meant. She strode on, glad to leave him behind. Half an hour later, they crested a small rise to find a wide gibber plain of purple and orange stone stretching before them. Mr. Pinkwhistle was hundreds of yards ahead, moving westward.

"I know you think Mr. Pinkwhistle is a top hunter, but I can't see how he's going to sniff out a motorcycle," said Callum, leaning over to rest his hands on his knees, trying to catch his breath.

"He will follow traces of your stink."

"I don't stink," said Callum.

Bo stepped close to him and leaned down to take in the scent of his skin. "You stink pretty," she said.

Callum drew away and clutched his shirt tightly against his sweaty chest. He looked out over the gibber plain to where Mr. Pinkwhistle was running in widening circles trying to pick up a trail. "I wish I could remember more. There were some spiky plants where I fell. I was lucky I didn't get pinned under the Daisy-May. The engine cut out. And then I walked for ages, heading over to that scrubby place where you found me. I don't know why I can't remember. I used to have a good instinct for lost things."

"Stink?"

"No, instinct—not 'stink.' Instinct—it's, you know, when you feel something instead of knowing it."

"Like 'twition?" asked Bo. "Woman's 'twition?"

Callum laughed. "What planet have you been living on, kid?"

Bo wasn't sure if she wanted to laugh along or pinch him. In awkward silence, they trudged across the plain toward a stretch of nubbly golden scrub. Mr. Pinkwhistle had disappeared but they could hear the sound of his whirring growl close by.

Finally they found the Daisy-May lying at the bottom of a small gully. Callum let out a whoop of pleasure and scrambled down to crouch beside it. Bo walked along the stony rise, cautiously checking the horizon before she joined him. Mr. Pinkwhistle sat on the Daisy-May's tank, his snout bobbing as a garbled victory cry rattled in his throat.

Bo squatted beside the bike and ran one hand over its pearly tank. "Gosh. Lovely."

Tipping her head to one side, she peered at the control panels. She traced her finger over the odometer and positioning devices, trying to get a sense of the machine's capabilities.

"We'll never get her started," said Callum. "I tried and tried, but nothing I did worked. She's too heavy for us to even lift."

Bo concentrated on the bike. Suddenly her hand found the control she'd been searching for, and the Daisy-May sent out a spike into the rocky ground and pushed itself upright.

"There," said Bo. "Fixed."

"No way. She's probably out of juice, too," said Callum. "Getting her upright isn't going to help if we can't get her going."

"Reserve," said Bo. She shut her eyes as she tried to remember how to explain herself. "One activates the reserve tank in emergencies. It allows one to travel short distances."

"It can't be that simple," Callum said. He jumped onto the bike, grabbed the handlebars, and gunned the accelerator. Nothing happened. Bo stood watching and tried not to look amused. She sensed it would only irritate him. He glanced over his shoulder at her. "What are you looking so smug for?"

"May I?" she asked.

"No. I need to think about it for a while."

Little beads of sweat ran down the side of Callum's neck as he fiddled with the switches and peered down the side of the bike to see if there was a way to kick-start it. After ten long, hot minutes he slumped in the seat and shrugged his shoulders.

"She's stuffed."

Silently, Bo swung one leg in front of the boy, nudging him onto the backseat. Mr. Pinkwhistle jumped onto the tank in front. Callum moved as far as he could along the seat, away from both of them.

"Hold tight," instructed Bo.

The Daisy-May roared to life and with a bone-shuddering jolt raced up the side of the gully and onto the gibber plain. The hot desert wind stung their skin, and the bike picked up speed so quickly that it was hard to breathe, but Bo loved it. She felt the boy draw closer and slide one arm around her shyly. Bo smiled into the wind.

8
The First Cut

That evening Callum sat watching as Bo took a bowl of crushed seed, mixed it into dough, and then buried the dough among hot coals at the back of the wood-fired oven.

"Aren't you worried someone will see the smoke?" he asked.

Bo smiled. It was a strange pleasure to have someone to talk to who could answer back. "One cannot see smoke clearly on moonless nights," she replied.

Callum crossed over to the burrow entrance, checking that the stone door was wedged tightly in place.

"No one is out there," said Bo.

"You can't know that," he said.

"We would hear them. Only I know how to cross the minefields."

"Then how did they kill your poppy? Was he your dad or your granddad? Or did he buy you? Those green eyes of yours, I've only seen them on chimeras. You talk funny, too."

Bo turned away from the boy. He made her brain feel scrambled. She wondered why, only a moment ago, she had been excited at the idea of conversation. Now she felt anger welling inside her, but she didn't know how to make it take shape.

"It is six months since I spoke to another human. The words come, but slowly. Six months since my Poppy died, my grandfather, my *blood* kin. We were hunting on the edge of the minefield. They came from nowhere. Outriders. One of them died crossing over. One of them murdered Poppy. The murderer did not find me. The walls of Tjukurpa Piti are too thick for Outriders to sense my presence."

"But they scout this territory, don't they? Could they force their way through your minefield? Do you have any allies? How can you protect yourself? How can you stop them from attacking?"

Bo put her hand over her ears. The boy's questions were like needles.

"If I read you another story, will you stop?"

Callum looked surprised but he nodded. "You have more stories?"

"Only if you have no more questions!"

"I liked that story about the boys who turned into ravens. Do you have another like that?"

Bo pulled a book from the shelf and settled herself on

the sofa with Mr. Pinkwhistle on her lap. "This is the story of 'The Wild Swans,' of Elisa and her eleven brothers."

As Bo began to read, Callum drew closer until finally he snuggled down beside her, peering over her shoulder to see the pictures of Elisa crushing nettles to make yarn for her brothers' fine shirts. When she finished "The Wild Swans," Bo read on. She read stories of brothers and sisters lost in dark forests, of snow queens and robber brides, until Callum's head rested sleepily on her shoulder.

When she was sure he was fast asleep and would ask no more infuriating questions, she slipped off the couch and picked up a catskin rug to cover him. The boy's ragged shirt had ridden up and Bo stared at the mass of welts and scars that covered his back. She looked at her own scars, the white criss-cross markings on her legs made by playful roboraptors, the old scars on her hands from small accidents with knives. They were nothing like the welts on this boy's body. Her scars mapped a good life at Tjukurpa Piti, each a sign of a skill she had gained, a lesson she had learned. Callum's scars were fresh, still glowing with a flush of pink where the skin was newly healed. He had learned his lessons from a harsh teacher. Tenderly, she laid the rug across the sleeping boy.

For the next two days, Callum wouldn't leave the burrow. Mostly he lay on the sofa and slept or watched Bo as she went through her daily routines: drawing water from the artesian well in the cave, salting and preserving cat meat, or threshing seeds from woollybutt grass that she gathered on her morning and evening hunts. Every few hours he rose from the sofa to check on the Daisy-May. Bo

45

had set the Wombator to work carving a new cave next to her workroom to house the motorcycle. She knew she would find Callum there whenever he wasn't asleep.

On the third night, when she returned to the burrow after her sunset hunt, she found the boy rummaging through the drawers in the kitchen.

"What do you search for?" she asked.

"This collar is driving me crazy. I'm going to cut it off." He pulled out one of her sharpest knives and held it against the ring of steel that encircled his neck.

"You will slice a vein if you try like that." Bo took the knife from him and pushed Callum onto the sofa. She ran her finger around the torque, searching for a hinge or rivet. When her hair brushed against his cheek, he squirmed.

"Be still," she said.

Using a small screwdriver and a length of wire, she picked the lock and unsnapped the hinge of the collar. As she pulled the torque away from Callum's neck, it let out a long singing wail of alarm. Bo dropped it in surprise. Mr. Pinkwhistle scurried out from beneath the kitchen table and took the ring in his teeth, chomping down hard, crushing the thick metal. A profusion of wires spilled from the torque. The wail stopped and Mr. Pinkwhistle trotted across to Bo and dropped the remnants at her feet.

"This has been sending out a signal ever since you arrived," she said, nudging the mess of metal and wire with her foot. A heavy, sick feeling settled in the pit of her stomach. She looked up to see Callum's face gray and drawn.

"Do not be afraid. Inside, we are safe," she said, desperate to believe it was true.

Callum picked up the broken remnants of his torque. "Not for long."

For the rest of the evening, Callum sat silently on the sofa, turning the torque over in his hands and brooding. Bo tried to ignore him as she secured the burrow for the night but his silence was like a cloud that filled every crevice of the cave.

It was nearly midnight when they heard the first explosion. It made the burrow shudder and Callum jump up in fright. The roboraptors scurried under the table.

"The minefield," said Bo. "Something's in the minefield."

They both held their breath, waiting for another explosion. When none came, Bo pulled Mr. Pinkwhistle onto her lap and opened up his chest. She checked the settings of his motion sensor. There were three men moving stealthily on the edge of her territory.

"They will not try again."

"Yes they will," said Callum. "They'll hunt me down, no matter what."

"Hunt you? Hunt for a boy?"

"Not only me. It's Daisy-May they're after. And this."

Callum pulled a battered leather wallet from his waistband and threw it onto the kitchen table. Bo picked it up, weighing it in her hands.

"Is this important?"

"Drugs. Gold. Gambling booty. That pee-wit, Dental,

thought he could do a runner on a brotherhood of gamblers. This was a whole night's takings."

Bo raised her eyebrows.

"Don't look at me like that. As if you don't believe me. I'm not some made-up boy like those kids in your books. This is the real world I'm talking about. I know how it works. They'll hunt us down the way you hunt those feral cats. They'll wait for us in the dark and then *pichewww—* we're dead meat, or worse."

"I am not afraid," said Bo.

"You should be. There are no kings or queens or fairies out there that are going to save you. I know what these people are like. There's only one thing we can do. Take the Daisy-May and try to outrun them."

"They will die in my minefield."

"Bo, those men are only Outriders. Even if they don't come back, more will follow. Every man in every outstation in the desert will come looking for me. Word travels. They'll know I have booty. They'll find this place one way or another. Your minefield won't protect us. And they won't care if you're innocent. They'll kill you or sell you."

Bo looked at the scrawny, scarred boy standing in her kitchen. Why hadn't she left him in the desert? Everything Poppy had worked for was jeopardized by his presence.

"You leave. I will stay. I will hide deep," said Bo.

"Don't you get it? You will be buried alive," said Callum. "They scorch it all."

Bo looked at him questioningly.

"They destroy everything. Make it so there's no point in coming back. Smash everything, poison the water, throw flame around so that everything's black, and then they piss on it so it stinks."

"This is an opal burrow," said Bo. "It will not burn."

"Then they'll blow it up," said Callum.

Bo checked Mr. Pinkwhistle's motion sensor again. "The Outriders have retreated. They have turned west. They are not coming this way."

Callum shook his head. "They'll be back."

9
A Rock and a Hard Place

Bo slept badly that night. She kept Mr. Pinkwhistle close to her and woke every hour to check his monitors. Even without looking, she could sense something evil drawing closer. She stood by Callum's sleeping body. He lay sprawled across her sofa, his mouth open, his tousled dark hair sticking out in all directions. He twitched in his sleep, one hand tucked under his cheek. He was like a wild bird, a carrier of disease, poisoning her nest. She was going to lose everything because of him and yet she didn't want to see him hurt or betray his trust. She rested her hand against his chest and felt the pulse of their two hearts beating.

Before dawn, Bo crept out to scan her territory. A pale silvery gray light rose over the eastern horizon and in the distance she could see the faint glimmer of men and machines searching for a path through the minefield.

Bo walked around the burrow, gently touching everything in the rooms. She stroked the shimmery stone walls. Then she herded the roboraptors out from beneath the kitchen table and down into the deepest burrow. They mewled and butted her ankles as they followed her into unfamiliar territory. When they could go no deeper, she set the herd in a row and stroked their smooth shells, chucked them each under the chin, and one by one set them to rest. But when she reached Mr. Pinkwhistle and saw his eyes glittering in the darkness, she couldn't bring herself to shut him down. She thought of all the times he had hunted for her, of his preternatural ability to understand what she needed. She tipped his jaw upward, opening the small cavity where his head joined his neck, then paused. She couldn't do it. Before she could change her mind, she opened the casing in his chest, punched in a new program, and led him back to the main living area.

Once she was at the top of the winding burrow, she set the Wombator to work, covering up the entrance to the herd's hiding place. If she couldn't protect them, she was determined that they would be safely entombed. They must never belong to Outstationers.

When the Wombator had completed the task, she took him into the southeast reaches of the burrow and programmed him to dig at his fastest setting. As the tunnels hummed with the vibrations of his burrowing, Bo began to pack. She pulled down two old cat-leather bags that Poppy had made and began weaving their handles together to make a pair of panniers to sling across the Daisy-May. She packed salted meat, bread, a bladder of water, and an assortment of items she thought might be useful for traveling. When everything was ready, she went to wake Callum.

She leaned over him and shook his shoulder. "You must go now."

"Huh?" said Callum, blinking. Bo shoved a slice of bread into his hands and put a catskin shawl around his shoulders.

"Traveling gear," she said in answer to his questioning expression. "You have to leave."

Callum sat up and rubbed his face with his hands. "Now?"

As he spoke, another landmine exploded, this time close enough to cause a shower of dirt to fall upon them. Callum shook the dust from his hair and followed Bo to where the Daisy-May stood waiting in the work cave. She could hear the faint whirr of the Wombator, and now, barely audible, the shouts of the approaching Outstationers. The Wombator came trundling back from the lower depths of the caves seeking new instructions.

Bo pointed a remote control at the dusty brown lump of synthetic fur and metal. Its tiny black eyes swiveled as she punched in the new set of directions. The Wombator turned its nose toward a corner of the cave and waddled away again, disappearing into the darkness.

"Since you came, he's been digging," said Bo. "To the southeast there are tunnels in an old mine, for many miles. He is digging a link. You will not be above ground until you are far, far away, so you will be safe. Safe from their eyes."

"But if it's a tunnel underground, how will we know where we're going?"

"The Daisy-May has many spiffing devices."

Bo blushed as Callum laughed at her words. "She has sensors," Bo continued. "One works on black body—like infrared—but she also has ultrasound and . . ." She started pushing buttons and the control panel of the motorcycle lit up like a Christmas tree ". . . some sort of radar. Made to pick up something . . . what's that word? Specific. She has a GPS, too."

"A what?"

"A global positioning system."

"They don't work anymore. Even I know that. The satellites blew when my dads were boys."

"This one works on magnetic fields."

She glanced up at Callum and saw that his expression had changed from amusement to quiet admiration.

"Where did you learn all this stuff?"

"My Poppy was an engineer," said Bo. She shut her eyes, remembering the last time she'd seen him, when he'd turned to face the Outstationers, defending her, as she would defend Callum.

"Scuttle," she said, repeating her grandfather's instructions. "You must scuttle."

As the words left her lips, another blast rocked the burrow.

"That was close," said Callum. "Closer than the last one."

Bo checked the supplies. She had strapped her home-made panniers to either side of the machine. In one of them sat Mr. Pinkwhistle, his shiny snout protruding from beneath the flap.

"Why bring him?" asked Callum.

"I may die fighting. You take Mr. Pinkwhistle with you. He must survive."

"What are you talking about?"

"First, I help you to escape. Then I return to defend my home."

"Come with me, Bo," said Callum. "You can't stay here." He gripped her by both shoulders. She couldn't meet his eye. Beneath her calmness, the breath was being squeezed from her lungs and her heart was pounding. Another blast shook the burrow. Behind them, the living area ceiling collapsed in a crushing roar of fallen rock.

"Bo! There is nothing to defend. You have to come with me—all the way."

Bo looked back at what was left of her kitchen. The oven had imploded, sending a plume of ash and rock into the air. The bookshelves and worn brown sofa were buried beneath a pile of rubble. The Outstationers were pounding against the roof, scrabbling at the rock, trying to force their way through. Her stomach ached and her feet felt as if they were made of lead but she snatched her string bag of hunting tools from a hook on the wall of the work cave and flung them into the panniers.

"Quickly. Help me push the Daisy-May until the Wombator breaks through, or the fumes will poison us."

Callum took up a position on one side of the motorcycle and they began to push the machine along the narrow passageway, into the darkness. Behind them, another explosion destroyed her work cave and they heard the sound of the Outstationers smashing their way through rock. Sweat dripped down Bo's forehead and into her eyes. She glanced across at Callum. He was struggling, too, his face tight with strain. She dug her toes deeper into the dirt and tried to take more of the weight of the bike. They heard another muffled thud and the air filled with dust. The caves behind them were collapsing, crushing her hopes.

Suddenly, the air grew clearer and Bo signaled for Callum to stop. She could just make out a flurry of movement ahead—the Wombator.

"He's broken through."

She swung one leg over the bike and gestured for Callum to climb on behind her. When his arms were wrapped tightly around her waist, she revved the accelerator. The Daisy-May sprang forward, its lights knifing through the darkness. Dust billowed around them as the bike picked up speed, hugging the tunnel's curves, winding deeper into the earth. Suddenly the tunnel opened out into caves where rusty brown stalactites hung from the ceiling. Bo could feel the shift in their progress. At last they were climbing upward. She dropped the Daisy-May down a gear and its wheels sent sprays of pelletty rock around their ankles.

They were both blinded by harsh sunlight as the Daisy-May broke the surface. The motorcycle surged out onto the desert plain like a wild animal released from a trap, fishtailing on the red soil. Bo swallowed the fresh air with relief. The empty wilderness spread out before them.

Bo drove the Daisy-May in and out of the low, scrubby trees scattered across the plain. The air quickly began to heat up as the sun rose higher, and she pushed the release for the shield so they were enclosed by the cool blue cover. She tried to hold on to the sense of elation she'd felt when they broke the surface, but deep inside her, a hollow place was growing with every mile that took her farther away from Tjukurpa Piti. The desert stretched to a distant horizon, waiting to swallow them both. From far away they could hear the sound of yet more explosions, and Bo knew her home was destroyed. She pictured Tjukurpa Piti, the roboraptors, the Wombator, all her possessions buried under falling rock and plumes of black smoke pouring into the desert sky. A gasping pain rose in her chest, as if she were spiraling away from all that was safe, lost in space.

As if he could read her thoughts, Callum leaned forward and spoke into her ear.

"Don't look back. Don't ever look back."

10
Last Girl Alive

Bo set the coordinates of the Daisy-May's GPS to the water hole. It was the only place outside Tjukurpa Piti that she had ever visited, the only place she knew of where they might be safe. She and Poppy had taken a week to drive there in his solar jeep, but the Daisy-May covered the distance in a matter of hours. The long, rugged mountain range came into view, purple in the distance. Up close, it loomed above them, a towering red. Once they drew near, Bo could read her way by studying every rock and twisted gum tree.

The entrance to the gorge was wide but then the high cliffs narrowed until the two children were enclosed in a red vault with only a strip of blue sky above. In front of them lay the water hole, its pale green surface dappled with shimmery light. Above, a breeze rippled through the leaves of trees edging the top of the gorge.

"It's beautiful, isn't it?" she said, turning to Callum.

She balanced Mr. Pinkwhistle on the tank of the Daisy-May and jumped down onto the sand. "Poppy brought me here to teach me to swim. We were happy here."

She stood on the banks of the water hole and was overcome by a desire to submerge her body in the cool green water, to wash away the dust of Tjukurpa Piti and her grief. In an instant, she had stripped off her clothes.

Callum gasped. "What happened to you?"

Bo looked down the length of her body, trying to see herself through his startled eyes. Her limbs were the same honey color they had always been. She swept her long hair over her shoulder and stared back at him.

"Nothing has happened."

"Have you always been like this?"

"Like what?"

"Did someone cut it off?"

"Cut what off?" she asked, raising her arms in a gesture of confusion.

"But you've got . . ." Callum climbed off the bike and took a step closer, leaning forward to peer at her torso. "It's sort of like a front bottom."

Bo pushed him away. "I do not have a front bottom!" she shouted. She stormed across the sandy bank and waded into the water until it lapped around her waist.

"Then what happened to you?" persisted Callum, calling to her from the bank.

Bo glanced at her reflection in the rippling water. She

folded her arms across her bare chest and spoke over her shoulder. "That's the way I was born. What's the matter with you? Haven't you ever seen a girl?"

"A girl?" Bo heard the incredulity in his voice and turned to face him. He was sitting on a rock, shivering.

"Callum?"

But he didn't answer. His eyes were wide and frightened. Bo realized he wasn't teasing.

"What is it?" she said, wading out of the water.

"Don't come any closer," he said, putting one hand out as if to ward her off. "I don't want to catch anything."

"From the water?"

"No, from you. If you really are a girl, then you might be toxic."

Bo stood before him, her fists clenched, fighting down her discomfort.

"You have been with me for days and you are alive and well. Why are you afraid?"

"When I was little, I thought maybe my dads made girls up to scare me," said Callum, averting his gaze as if the sight of Bo's nakedness was too appalling to confront. "I can't believe I've been with you this long and not realized. I knew you were different but . . ."

Slowly, he turned to face her. "Now I understand why you made that joke about 'woman's 'twition.' I laughed. I didn't think anyone had any women's anything. But you weren't joking, were you?"

"Why would it be a joke?"

"Women are extinct."

"Extinct? Like your instinct?"

"No, that's different. *Extinct* means completely gone. Like dinosaurs. There are no more dinosaurs, only fake ones like Mr. Pinkwhistle. And there are no more women."

Bo lapsed into silence and pushed her toe into the sand.

"I feel like I'm dreaming," said Callum, edging away from her. "I've heard men say they believed that somewhere in the world girls still exist, that someone would discover one some day. My dads said it was crazy, like imagining fossils can come back to life. Dinosaurs, dodos, girls . . . they're meant to be ancient history."

Bo sat down beside Callum. "I'm flesh and bones. Like you. Not a fossil." She reached out for one of his hands. He had jammed them both into his armpits and she could feel his resistance but she persisted, tugging one free and then putting her palm against his, forcing him to touch her. "See, we both have exactly five fingers. Mine are a little longer than yours. Your hands are a little wider. But they're the same. Two hands."

Then she put her foot beside his. "Same feet, too, except yours are like flippers. Bigger than mine!" Lastly, she took his hand and pushed it against her chest. "Feel that? That is my heart beating. Same as yours. I listened to your heart when you were sleeping. You have a strong rhythm. A good heart."

Callum kept the flat of his palm against her bare chest, his face growing still as he felt her heartbeat. He stared at her, his dark eyes puzzled. "I thought when you read me those stories with girls in them that they were fantasy. But you're like one of those princesses or witches or fairies. Except you must be the last. The last girl alive."

They stood staring at each other warily. Their silence hung above the swimming hole. Bo flung a pebble into the water and the ripples spread in widening circles. Poppy had told her that her mother and grandmother had died in the plague. He never told her that every girl had perished. She turned Callum's words over and over in her mind. Then she pointed to the end of the swimming hole where the gorge narrowed.

"Sometimes animals fall into the gorge. When we came last time, I saw a dead kangaroo floating. It must have washed down into the swimming hole. I thought it was alive, the way it moved in the water, but when I swam out it was only a big, stinky carcass. Things are not always as they seem."

"So what are you trying to tell me? Are you saying that you're like a stinking carcass?"

Bo's smile fell away. She ran into the water and freestyled into the gorge, all the way to where a small cascade of water broke out of the high wall. She dove deep, trying to ignore the fact that Callum was calling her name. She swam until her lungs were bursting and she was finally forced to come up for air.

When she surfaced and looked back, the look of relief on Callum's face made her laugh.

"I thought you'd drowned," he shouted.

Bo did a leisurely backstroke and pretended to ignore him. He looked hot and miserable, sitting on the edge of the water hole with his arms wrapped tightly around his knees, watching her as she swam.

"Come into the water," she called.

"No."

"Are you still afraid of me?"

Callum kicked a spray of sand into the water. "Yes and no."

"If no, then come and swim with me."

"I don't know how to swim."

Bo waded back onto the shore and reached for his hands.

"I am going to prove to you that girls aren't scary," she said, pulling him to his feet. She held his face between her hands and stared straight into his eyes. "And I will show you that girls have their uses. Take off your clothes. I am going to teach you how to swim."

Callum let out an exhausted sigh. Slowly, he stripped away his tattered clothes until he was standing naked before her. He didn't look at her body, only her face. Then he held out his hands. Bo smiled and slowly led him into the water, until it was lapping around their waists. "Are you frightened?" she asked.

Callum nodded. She stepped behind him and, very gently, pulled him toward her. "Then I think you are brave. Because these are two things you are afraid of, water and girls, and yet both of them are touching you. So now you are going to show you are truly courageous and let me hold you."

When she slipped her arm around his waist and tried to

make him bend, his body was stiff and unyielding. "Relax. I promise you are safe."

She lifted Callum off his feet so that his legs floated free and then walked slowly backward into deeper water until his whole body was afloat. She kept his head resting on her shoulder, their cheeks touching, as she moved deeper into the gorge. Callum's golden limbs floated just beneath the surface of the swirling green water.

For a moment Bo wanted to cry out in wonder, it looked so strange and beautiful to see another human moving like a free-falling angel through the watery space. Instead she spoke to him in a low, soft voice, explaining that he was safe, she wouldn't let him go, he could relax and let the water and her arms support him. Then she drew him back to shore.

Callum opened his eyes when his feet touched the sandy bottom. They sat together in the shallows, their eyes mirroring the sunlight sparkling on the water hole.

Callum wiped his arms and smiled as another layer of dirt sloughed from his skin. "I feel so clean," he said. "I feel all new."

"When you're in this gorge, the rest of the world falls away. There is nothing but this moment. We could stay here for as long as we want."

"We definitely can't stay here," said Callum. "They'll track us, Bo. It's not just me that I'm worried about. It's you. We can't let them catch you. I bet Outstationers have never seen a girl before either. Not a real one. They'll put you in a freak show."

"I'm not a freak. I'm a girl."

"Don't you understand? That's freaky. Being a girl is . . . weird."

Bo wriggled uncomfortably, as if her skin no longer fit her lanky bones.

Callum knelt close to her, talking with a new urgency. "We have to go and find my dads. I promise, if we find them, you'll be safe. They'll take care of both of us. You could be my sister, like in those stories you read to me. Brother and sister. As long as it's legal to have a sister."

Bo shut her eyes. "I don't need anyone to take care of me. I take care of myself."

"How? You can't go home."

"Neither can you."

Callum slapped the water, sending droplets into the air. "That's not true! Even if the Outstationers did destroy the Refuge, my dads would build it again. It's not like your place. There's no one to rebuild Tjukurpa Piti. But my dads work for the Colony. The Refuge was an important outpost. Ruff and Rusty will be back there, rebuilding and waiting for me."

"There are yams and berries here. There is water. I have my hunting tools and Mr. Pinkwhistle."

"Are all girls born stupid?" Callum shouted. "Is that why they were wiped out? Or is it just you?"

Bo got silently to her feet and dived into the water hole, swimming to the far side of the gorge. She rinsed her hair under the waterfall and let the sound of the cascade drown out Callum's voice. When she finally swam out into the open gorge, she could hear Callum shouting, "Get out, get out of the water!"

"Leave me alone," she shouted back.

"No, listen to me! Something's coming. Something bad."

Bo turned to see what he was pointing at and saw a long, rippling darkness coming toward her. She made it to the shore as quickly as she could and pushed Callum away from the water's edge. Snatching up her discarded clothes, she ran to the Daisy-May. Callum climbed onto the bike expectantly but Bo snapped her fingers to activate Mr. Pinkwhistle and he leaped from the pannier. The roboraptor turned his head toward Bo, his eyes glowing with a soft green light as he scanned the gorge. Bo drew a long knife and a pistol from inside her string bag.

"Wait. Don't move. Don't make a sound. You are bait."

Callum stared at her, his mouth open, but he stayed put. Bo stroked the underside of Mr. Pinkwhistle and then, quick as a lizard, she scrambled up the side of the gorge until she was on a rock overhanging the water's edge. When the crocodile finally emerged from the water hole, she took aim.

Mr. Pinkwhistle stood between Callum and the crocodile, emitting a low, whirring growl. Distracted, the crocodile turned its huge snout toward the roboraptor and opened its mouth. Bo fired one direct shot to the back of its skull and the reptile slumped on the shore, twitching. She scrambled down from the rock and pulled a long metal spike out of one of the bike panniers. Sitting astride the crocodile's body, she shoved the spike through its skull at the point where the bullet had entered. Then she dragged the carcass away from the water's edge and squatted down beside it.

"Are you sure it's dead?" Callum stayed on the far side of the Daisy-May.

Bo didn't bother to answer. She flipped the reptile over and cut a long incision into its belly, working her knife all the way down to its tail.

"This will make a delicious dinner. White meat is sweeter than pudding."

Callum screwed up his face. "Meat doesn't taste sweet. Pudding, donuts, chocolate—now that's sweet. Not crocodile meat."

"Have you ever eaten it before?"

This time it was Callum's turn to stay silent.

Bo concentrated on the task at hand. When she'd cut away the flesh from the tail and belly and wrapped it in a damp cloth, she shoved the parcel into Callum's arms. Next she dragged the butchered carcass away from the water hole and out of the gorge, leaving it on a stretch of flat desert ground.

"What are you doing?" he called after her.

"It must not foul the water hole," she called to Callum over her shoulder.

Callum stood holding the parcel of meat awkwardly away from his body as he perched on the back of the Daisy-May.

"It doesn't matter if it fouls the water hole," he said. "We're not staying. It's too dangerous."

Bo took the parcel from him.

"It can't bite you now. We are safe."

"Safe? We will never be safe until we find my fathers."

"I can protect you."

Callum flushed darkly and scowled. "Protect me? You made me bait. And now Mr. Pinkwhistle has turned on me, too."

Bo looked down and realized Mr. Pinkwhistle was crouching as if to attack, watching Callum with sharp intent. She bent down and lifted the roboraptor with her free arm. Immediately, he stopped growling and began to nuzzle her chin with his snout.

"Why was he doing that?" asked Callum.

"He's programmed to sense emotion as well as movement. He understands you are frightened, so he thinks you are dangerous, or maybe good to hunt. But he will never harm you. I would not allow anyone to hurt you. You have nothing to worry about."

"Frankly, I think we both have a lot to worry about," said Callum. He walked away from her to dress in private. Then he sat down on the sandy bank and put his head in his hands.

Bo stood up, shook the dust from her catskin clothes, and put them on. They clung to her wet skin but she was glad to be dressed. She gathered her weapons and packed them into the panniers. Then she swung a leg over Daisy-May and carefully positioned Mr. Pinkwhistle on the tank in front of her. "Where is this place you seek? Your fathers' Refuge."

Callum glanced over his shoulder and grunted. "I don't know how to get there."

"We will find it. Mr. Pinkwhistle and the Daisy-May will show us the way."

Callum blinked in surprise. "We're going? Is it that easy to make a girl change her mind?"

"No," said Bo, laughing. "Sometimes, what you say makes sense. If you have a home to go to, that's where you should be."

Callum jumped onto the back of the Daisy-May. He wrapped his arms around Bo and rested his cheek against her back. She drove the Daisy-May slowly out of the gorge and kept the shield down so the desert wind dried her hair. Then she pushed the release button and the two of them were cocooned again inside the blue darkness of the shield. The Daisy-May skimmed over the desert, until the landscape was a blur on either side of them and the journey ahead was all that Bo could focus on. She had lost her Poppy, she had lost her home and all her herd but for Mr. Pinkwhistle. But she had found this boy, and when he put his arms around her, she knew she had found a reason to go on.

11
The Wreck of the Refuge

It took them two days to reach the Refuge. Or what was left of it. From a distance, Bo spotted a tall white pole with an oval sign on top and faint writing in dull solar neon. As they drew closer it was clear that the sign said Ruff & Rusty's Roadside, but the last word had been seared by flame and was unreadable. Callum's home was nothing but a heap of dust and ash. Low scrub and sandy, red-gold desert stretched as far as the eye could see to the pale purple haze on the far horizon, uninterrupted by any type of man-made shelter.

Callum gripped Bo as they drew nearer.

"Squeeze me any tighter and I will stop breathing," she said.

Callum loosened his grasp but Bo could still feel his fear growing. As soon as the hood of the Daisy-May slid open, he jumped off the bike and ran into the midst of the wreckage.

Bo lifted Mr. Pinkwhistle from his pannier, and they followed Callum across the ruined site. He squatted in the center of what had once been a kitchen, cradling a mangled figurine in one hand and a soup ladle in the other. The sun beat down on them, scorching their faces.

"They didn't come back," he said disbelievingly. "I thought they'd camp out, wait to see if I came home. I thought they'd do anything to find me."

"You've been gone for months," said Bo.

"They still should have waited."

"Maybe they followed the circus, hoping to buy you back?"

Callum turned on her. "You don't understand anything, do you? My dads had no way of knowing where I would wind up. But they could have waited. They were my fathers. They shouldn't have given up!" he shouted, his face contorted with rage and grief.

Bo walked back to the Daisy-May. She sat in the shade and watched Callum picking through the wreckage in a desultory way. She settled Mr. Pinkwhistle on her lap and flipped open his chest to program new instructions. "We have to help him, Mr. P."

Mr. Pinkwhistle set off at a trot, his head gyrating and his beady eyes flashing red to green as he surveyed the site. At the base of the solar sign, he stopped and pawed the ground. Bo knelt down beside him.

"We've found something," she called.

Wearily, Callum trudged toward her, kicking aside piles of ash and debris.

"Look at this," she said, pointing to where Mr. Pinkwhistle was bobbing up and down beside a dusty patch of earth.

"What?" he said flatly.

"Someone has been here. Mr. Pinkwhistle has a tracker facility. He's magnified and interpreted these markings. It shows humans camped on this spot." She knelt down beside Mr. Pinkwhistle and flicked open a panel on his back to reveal a small monitor. "At least two, maybe three men. They were here for a while but they left more than a month ago. Maybe your fathers waited, just as you said they would."

Callum looked at her with glazed eyes and shook his head.

"They still gave up on me," he said, sitting down beside her on the hot ground.

"What's that?" she asked, gently taking the twisted figurine from his hand.

"He was our Elvis cuckoo clock man," said Callum. "He used to jump out and sing 'Heartbreak Hotel' every hour." He wiped his hands across his eyes. "I guess my dads thought he wasn't worth keeping."

"Maybe they left you a message," suggested Bo. "Maybe they wrote you a note and left it somewhere."

Callum shrugged and bit his lip. "They don't do that in my family. Leave messages."

"Why not?"

Callum said nothing and they sat together in mournful silence. Mr. Pinkwhistle continued to circle the solar sign-post, stopping to scratch at the dirt every few feet. Suddenly he let out a guttural chuckle.

"He's found something else!" said Bo. Mr. Pinkwhistle tipped his head back and chortled as he danced a victory dance at the base of the Refuge's signpost.

Bo and Callum stared at the patch of red earth and then at the post.

"Was all this writing on the pole before you left?"

Callum stood beside her and stared at the fading, scratchy marks. "I don't remember. What do they mean?"

Bo knelt beside the pole and ran her hands over the words. *If anyone passing knows the whereabouts of Callum Caravaggio, eleven-year-old métis Eurasian, brown eyes, black hair, wide smile, please contact R&R Caravaggio at Nehkbet Tower, Apartment 217, Vulture's Gate. Reward.*

"Vulture's Gate?" said Callum. "They've gone back to Vulture's Gate?"

"Where is that?"

"It's where the Colony was founded. When I was little, we lived in an apartment in a tower block there. I liked it. Other men and boys lived there, too. Then Ruff and Rusty took the contract for this place and we moved. They said it would be better to bring up a kid away from there."

"Why?"

"A long time ago, it was a good place to live, but the plague changed it. That's when it became Vulture's Gate, once the women died out."

"Do women still die there? Are there still birds?" asked Bo.

"Of course there are birds. But I told you, women are extinct. And Vulture's Gate is so far away, over on the east coast. Why did they have to go so far!"

Bo looked out over the wreckage of the Refuge. "There wasn't anything to keep them here."

"There was me!" shouted Callum, slamming the white post with his hand.

Bo didn't look at him but pointed at the sign. "That last symbol. What does it mean?"

Callum peered closer at the little illustration beneath the writing. It was of a hovering bird. "That's their way of letting me guess about Vulture's Gate, I suppose. I never cracked the reading thing but I always liked the symbol they taught me for Vulture's Gate."

"And these?" asked Bo, pointing to a little trail of arrows and circles that ran down the side of the pole like hieroglyphics.

Callum grinned. He knelt at the base of the pole, where Mr. Pinkwhistle had danced, and began scrabbling with his bare hands at the dry red earth. Bo knelt beside him and helped.

It was only 8 inches beneath the ground—a sealed metal box. They lifted it out together and dusted off the surface. There was a digital lock on the front but Callum knew the code and in an instant he had the lid open. Inside was a bag of donuts, dried-food parcels, six bottles of water, two packets of rehydration salts, a small roll of gold, and a toy penguin.

Callum snatched up the toy and hugged it. "I can't believe it! Peggy! She survived!" He laid the penguin in his lap and gently touched its belly where a small digital device was neatly embedded. The screen lit up and two men stared out. Bo peered over Callum's shoulder as the digital message began to play.

Callum pointed at each of the men. "The one with smooth black hair, that's Ruff. And the one with the thick reddish beard, that's Rusty." He turned up the volume so their voices reverberated across the desolate site.

"Callum, if you're listening to this, you'll know we came back to find you," said Rusty. "We bribed Outriders, we interrogated Outstationers, but we lost your trail. We've waited three weeks, hoping for news of you, but we can't stay longer. The Colony don't want to rebuild the Refuge so we're going back to Vulture's Gate." He began to cry. "Cal, darling, we will never give up hope. We'll come back to the west when we can, to search. But if you hear this and you have any way of getting word to us, know that we'll come running for you, son."

Callum played the message over and over again until Bo could mime every word his fathers spoke and she longed for him to turn it off. Finally, he tore open the bag of donuts and handed one to Bo. "I knew they wouldn't give up on me," he said, crowing between mouthfuls.

Bo took a bite of her donut and spat it into the dirt.

"What are you doing?" asked Callum, snatching the treat away from her.

"It tasted strange. It made my teeth tingle. That crunchy white stuff, it burns."

"That's sugar. And it tastes fantastic," said Callum, through a crowded mouthful. "This is the sort of food those kids in your storybooks eat all the time. Not crocodile and weeds."

Cautiously, Bo leaned forward and took another small bite from the ring of sugar and dough that Callum held in his fist. She scrunched up her nose in distaste and Callum laughed. He stuffed the rest of the donut into his mouth and dusted sugar from his fingers.

"Callum, I think we should go now," said Bo. "There's nothing else here."

"I want to camp until they come back."

"We can't," said Bo. "There is no shelter, no good hunting, and it's too close to the road."

Callum bowed his head and played the iPenguin message again, holding the small toy close to his face and studying his fathers' images. Bo remembered the way she had gazed at Poppy's picture, hopelessly longing for him. But it was different for Callum. His fathers were alive. Somewhere, out there, they were waiting for him.

"If only the old-tech ways still worked, we could get a message to them," he said. "But everything's broken. It's hopeless." He glanced around the barren landscape and the wreck of his old home. "I don't know how to reach them."

"I do," said Bo. "We're going to deliver the message ourselves. We're going to Vulture's Gate."

12
Evil Angels

Callum watched Bo from across the campfire. He didn't understand her. He'd always imagined that girls must have been sickly, unreliable creatures that spent a lot of time screaming and crying. But Callum hadn't seen Bo cry once and he couldn't help but trust her.

Now as he pushed at the coals with a stick, he felt something kindling deep inside, a beacon of hope rising from the wreckage of his old life. Bo drew a map in the dry desert soil, and using the GPS in Daisy-May and the notes that Callum's dads had left in the security box, she mapped out a route across the continent to the city on the far east coast.

"The Daisy-May runs on cactus juice," she said. "She has a mini-still built into her so we can feed her and make some fuel. But I don't know if she will get us all the way across the country. We need to find succulents for her every day."

Callum looked down at the map in the dust. Then he turned on the iPenguin and watched his fathers' message again. "We have to make it. With or without the Daisy-May."

The next morning, Callum packed what useful things he'd managed to salvage from the ashes of the Refuge. He made sure Peggy the iPenguin was stored in the pannier opposite Mr. Pinkwhistle and tucked the other things in around her. He didn't like the way the raptor swiveled his skull-like head toward Peggy and bared his shiny, sharp teeth every time Ruff and Rusty's message played.

Callum didn't look back as the Daisy-May sped away from the Refuge but he knew that part of who he used to be was behind him in the ashes, the best of his childhood lost to him. He hooked his arms tightly around Bo. Even if she was a girl, he knew she understood what it meant to lose your home.

The road through the desert ran like a long black crack across the landscape. The Daisy-May flew over the weathered bitumen, as if barely making contact. The terrain began to change quickly, drifts of red sand blowing across the road. They traveled at such speed that every day yielded new terrain. Every evening they foraged for succulents for the Daisy-May's still before curling up on their catskin rugs to sleep.

One evening, a week after they'd left the Refuge, they camped by a salt lake. It was covered by a thin sheen of water that shimmered orange and blood red at sunset. Bo cooked up the last of the dried crocodile meat, salting it with lake water.

After eating they lapsed into a companionable silence, but when the moon rose and the first nightbird of the evening wheeled overhead, Bo looked up from the campfire and frowned. Grabbing her string bag of weapons, she walked away from the camp and smoothed out a section of earth, clearing rocks and debris with the butt of her gun. Then she lay down on the ground and gazed up at the swirling, starry night sky.

"What's wrong?" called Callum.

"Shush, they'll hear you," she said in a loud whisper. "They're dangerous."

Callum tiptoed over and lay down beside her, mystified by her fear. Their shoulders touched and he felt that peculiar rush of blood that being close to Bo triggered in him. The desert earth beneath them was cool, but beside him Bo's skin felt as though it was shimmering with heat.

"What are you thinking?" he asked.

Bo didn't answer right away. She kept staring up at the stars, as if she were searching for something.

"What are you thinking?" she echoed.

"I've told you, you can't answer questions with questions. I wasn't thinking anything. I'm not always thinking. Sometimes I'm just being. You're the one that's lying there with a gun."

Bo shifted her shoulders, making a little space between her and Callum but he moved closer so they were touching again. He took hold of her hand and held it tightly.

"You must be easy to pick up with a heat sensor. Mr. Pinkwhistle's internal screens must light up fierce when he sees you."

As he spoke, Callum became even more aware of the patch of skin where their bodies met, the way their fingers meshed. He gazed up at the nightbird that hovered over their heads. Suddenly, Bo pulled her hand free of his grasp and raised her gun, staring hard into the night sky.

"What are you going to do? Shoot the stars?"

"No, the nightbirds," said Bo.

"Nightbirds! We can't eat them, they're too stringy."

"They are not for eating. Only killing."

Callum sat up. "My dads used to take me outside to watch them fly over the Refuge. Rusty said they only flew at night, because people had gone on crazy killing sprees when the plague happened so the birds learned to stop flying during the day. But they can't hurt us anymore, Bo. And they're beautiful. It's wrong to kill beautiful things. See, they look like black angels."

"They're not angels. They're evil." She lifted the gun, took aim, and fired.

Callum ran to where the wide-winged creature lay bleeding in the dust.

"Don't touch it!" shouted Bo. "Poppy said never to touch birds. They're poisonous. You should never eat them, or their eggs. Never touch anything they've touched. I used to have the Wombator bury them for me. And I never touched him. Poppy said everything with wings is dangerous."

"That's old superstition. No one gets the plague now."

"But you said there are no women. No girls. They were the ones that died."

"Are you afraid of birds?"

"I'm not afraid. I shoot them because they're evil. All winged creatures are horrible," she said. "They make a fluttering noise and it fills your head until you feel mad and tortured. Wings make my flesh creep."

Callum left the corpse and lay back down beside her without speaking. Bo clung grimly to her pistol but when another nightbird wheeled overhead, she didn't fire. He didn't know what to say to her. She seemed foreign again but also forlorn. He turned and put his face near hers so they were almost touching. Then he blinked slowly, his long eyelashes brushing against her cheek.

"What are you doing?" she asked.

"Giving you a butterfly kiss."

"What is a butterfly?"

"It's a tiny insect with soft wings. That was meant to feel like the brush of its wings."

Bo put a hand to her cheek. "Why did you do that?"

"Not everything with wings is horrible."

At dawn, the salt lake was coppery pink. For the first time since they had met, Callum woke before Bo. He sat up and scanned the lake. There was something moving across its surface, as if walking or gliding on the water. He blinked and realized it was Mr. Pinkwhistle. What was he doing up before Bo? He never went anywhere before she activated him for the day. Then Callum realized the roboraptor had something in his jaws and was shaking it, as if trying to snap it in two. Suddenly, Ruff and Rusty's voices drifted across the lake.

"Peggy!" shouted Callum. "He's killing Peggy!"

Bo was beside him in an instant, rubbing sleep from her eyes. She whistled for the roboraptor and he came skittering across the pink lake, sending thousands of flecks of silvery water into the air.

"Bad!" she shouted as he skidded to a stop in front of them. "Bad food!"

In his mouth were the mangled remains of Peggy the iPenguin. Fragments of Ruff and Rusty's voices squeaked out of her interface and then they stopped altogether.

"Drop!" said Bo. But it was too late. One of Peggy's glass eyes dangled from its socket and a long, thick wad of stuffing fell from her body. The interface in her belly was completely shattered. Callum stared down in horror at the tangled mess. Mr. Pinkwhistle's long tail swished back and forth, as if he was pleased with himself.

"I'm sorry," said Bo.

Callum couldn't tell her it was all right because it wasn't. Peggy was the last token of his lost childhood and now she was gone. He turned away and trudged back to the campsite. He didn't want Bo to see him cry.

He barely noticed when Bo came up behind him and touched his shoulder. She didn't say anything but she stood close to him. Gently, she took his head in her hands. When their faces were almost touching, she brushed his cheek with her eyelashes, a butterfly kiss that swept away the last of his tears.

13
The Hidden Valley

Callum kept a close eye on Daisy-May's sensors and while Bo focused on the road, he watched to make sure they were safe. When the monitors indicated another vehicle approaching, he tapped Bo on her thigh. She steered the bike off the road so they could wait in sheltering scrub for the strangers to pass. It slowed their progress and days slipped into weeks but they didn't want to risk making contact with anyone. Red sand was replaced by sandy yellow soil. Occasional gum trees began to pepper the roadside. Finally the country turned from desert scrub to forest.

One warm afternoon after a long day of travel, they found a sheltered, dry riverbed in which to camp. Bo lifted Mr. Pinkwhistle out of the pannier and set him on a rock to soak up the last of the day's sunlight before sending him out to hunt. Callum was anxious that they start scouring the surrounding country for succulents to feed the Daisy-May's still and was glad to see the roboraptor disappear into the scrub.

They returned to camp as darkness fell with only a small string bag of plants, to find Mr. Pinkwhistle waiting for them, pawing the ground miserably and loudly gnashing his metal teeth. He'd been unable to catch anything for their dinner and he let out a whirr of embarrassment when Bo stroked his spine.

When Mr. Pinkwhistle was calm again, Bo pulled the top from her water flask and licked the last drops from its rim. Then she flopped down in the sand and stretched out on her back. "I don't think we'll make it at this rate. We'll starve before we reach the city."

"When we get to Vulture's Gate, there'll be plenty of food," said Callum. "My dads will make sure of that. The Colony has storehouses full of stockpiled food."

"But we've still got hundreds of miles to go and we've almost no food and no water. We spend so much time traveling or looking for plants for the still that we don't have any time to find food. Mr. Pinkwhistle can't do all the hunting by himself. We need to stop and make camp for a while."

"No way! We have to keep moving!"

Bo sighed and pulled Mr. Pinkwhistle onto her lap. She opened up his chest and checked his sensors as she spoke. "Didn't you say your fathers used to *buy* supplies? Isn't that what people who can't hunt do? You've got gold. We should use it to purchase something."

"Who from? Outstationers? You think we can simply pull up at an outstation and trade? They would eat us for breakfast. We're probably a gazillion miles from any Colony outposts. There was one my dads used to go to on business. It was an old port, so stuff came to it from the sea. But it was bad news. Heaps of pirates and cutthroats. I was never allowed out of the Colony compound when we went there. You wouldn't want to walk around somewhere like that with a fistful of gold. Like I said, we have to do this alone. We can't trust anyone."

When he looked across at Bo, he realized she had stopped listening and was busy studying Mr. Pinkwhistle's sensors.

"Look at this," she said, pointing at a luminous glowing circle on the monitor.

"What's it mean?"

"It's a big body of water, maybe a dam or lake, but there are tanks as well. And some sort of power source. That means there must be people there. Not ordinary Outstationers or anyone like that Dental and Floss. Whoever is up there, they're jolly well organized. But there's something peculiar about it. I can't see any movement."

Suddenly the screen went dark and the green light disappeared. Mr. Pinkwhistle let out a low growl and shifted from one foot to the other, leaving a trail of little red scratches on Bo's thigh.

"Something's blocked the signal, but I did get a fix on where it is. It's a valley, inside a circle of hills somewhere over that way," she said, gesturing into the darkness. "I can put the coordinates into the Daisy-May and we could be there and back again in no time. If there's water, there should be good hunting. At least we could fill our flasks."

Callum frowned and rested his hands on his grumbling stomach. "What if there's someone there? It could be dangerous."

"We won't know unless we check it out."

The next morning they followed a winding trail up the side of a mountain. As they rode closer to the top, the path became heavily overgrown.

"This is taking us nowhere," said Callum. "We'll never get the Daisy-May through this scrub."

"Maybe we could climb to the top of the hill and just see if there really is anything down there. I don't understand why neither Mr. Pinkwhistle nor the Daisy-May has readings on it anymore. It's as if there's a blanket across the whole valley. Something about this place gives me the willies. It's claustrophobic. All this green. It's suffocating."

"It might be a Colony outpost. They can do things like that, blanket signals and all."

They parked the Daisy-May in the shelter of trees and covered her with brush. Bo slung her string bag over her shoulder and set Mr. Pinkwhistle down on the ground so he could scoot ahead of them, forging his way through thick ferns. As the bush grew denser, Callum's hope that the valley might be a Colony outpost flickered and died. There were no border guards, no fences, nothing but wilderness as far as the eye could see.

When they reached the crest of the hill, Bo climbed onto a high rock to survey the valley. For a moment she was silhouetted against the blue and then she crumpled, screaming. A flock of white cockatoos swept down from the sky and surrounded her, tearing her hair, and pecking until they drew blood. She huddled in a ball, paralyzed with terror.

Callum jumped up beside her and tried to bat the birds out of the way. "Hit them, Bo. Hit back!" he shouted.

Why didn't she fight? How could she be so courageous about everything else but let birds defeat her? Clumsily, he caught a cockatoo by its feet and used it to beat the others away. They shrieked and dove harder in a rush of feathers and wings, pecking his face and arms until they bled. Flecks of blood splattered their white wings. Suddenly, a thunderous noise dispersed the flock. Callum turned, still clutching a squawking cockatoo by its feet.

"Let go of the bird, sonny," said their rescuer, squinting through the viewfinder of his gun. "Let her go or I'll shoot you right through your nasty little heart."

14
Mollie Green

Callum released the bird and it flapped away to join the rest of the flock. Slowly, with one arm still raised in surrender, he reached down to Bo and helped her to her feet. She was trembling and her face was drawn and pale.

"You boys, you're trespassing," barked the hunter. "How'd you find your way to my valley?"

"We didn't mean any harm," said Callum.

The hunter lowered his gun and eyed them warily.

"You're pretty young to be wandering alone. You got men with you?" he asked, narrowing his eyes and scanning the bush.

"No, only us two," said Bo, her voice still shaky from the shock of the bird attack. "I'm Bo and this is Callum."

Callum elbowed her sharply in the ribs but she ignored him.

"Tell him nothing," he whispered into her ear. "He's not a Colony man."

"He saved us," replied Bo, turning back to the hunter.

Callum didn't like the look of him. He had a thick cloud of frizzy silver hair tied back in a ponytail, a long beard, and a dark, nut brown face. There was something wild in his pale eyes and his mouth was down-turned in a bitter expression.

"We need only water and fuel," said Bo. "Cactus juice for a peyote-bike. Enough to reach Vulture's Gate."

"We're not asking for favors," added Callum. "We can pay you."

"Money's no use to me," said the old man, spitting at Callum's feet. There was a long silence, and then Bo stepped forward and held her hands out, her palms turned upward.

"Please, sir," she said. "We shall be terribly grateful. Please."

"Long time since I've heard anyone say please," said the old man. "Thought that word had gone out of the dictionary." He looked them up and down and then spat again onto the rocks. "Hand over all your weapons and we'll do a deal. I've got a still. Make me own juice from corn. Power most of me engines with it. Should work for a peyote-bike."

Callum grabbed Bo by the arm and pulled her back as she unhitched the knife and pistol from her belt. "Don't give them to him. Let's keep going."

"We can't keep going if the Daisy-May hasn't any juice and we have no water."

"Then set Mr. Pinkwhistle on him," whispered Callum. "We'll jump him while he's distracted, tie him up, and steal what we need."

"No. That's not fair. He looks like my Poppy. I'm sure he won't hurt us," said Bo, pulling free. She turned to the old man, offering up her string bag. Callum wanted to slap her.

"I have a roboraptor as well but I'm not handing him over," she said. "He's too precious." She whistled and Mr. Pinkwhistle came loping out of the bush to stand beside her. The old man stared at the roboraptor in surprise.

"What on earth is that?"

"My grandfather made him. He's a biomechanical robotic predator. We hunt together."

"Do you have to tell him everything?" exclaimed Callum.

"Your mate is doing the right thing," said the hunter. "I like a boy who's upfront. Means I can trust him."

He knelt down beside Mr. Pinkwhistle and studied him closely. Callum wished the roboraptor would attack. "He was a clever man, your grandfather. I worked on trying to revive robotic slugs when I was young but the know-how was lost. I've got a Slugbot on my workbench and all he does is sit there. Never thought you could improve on the remnant technology."

The old man stood up again, using his rifle like a walking stick, as if his limbs ached.

"Now, I used to make kids call me Mr. Green. But you can call me Mollie if you like and we'll get down to business. Show me this bike of yours and I'll see if I can help you out."

Bo led the way over the hill to where the Daisy-May lay hidden in the bush. Callum couldn't believe how stupidly she was behaving. There was no way of knowing whether they could trust this man. Within minutes of finding the bike, Bo and Mollie were engaged in a serious conversation about mechanics while Callum stood by, quietly fuming.

After she had explained the workings of the Daisy-May to Mollie, they climbed down into the hidden valley. They passed through thick stands of bamboo, a clump of banana palms, an orchard crowded with low apple trees, and finally a long stand of trellises covered by vines heavy with exotic fruit. By the time they reached the bottom of the valley, Callum's mouth was watering.

They came to a small village of bark-and-timber huts surrounded by a bank of solar panels with a windmill spinning busily above the roofs. Mollie Green pushed open the door to one of the huts and gestured for the children to come inside.

While Bo followed Mollie into the hut, Callum stayed near the door, looking around warily.

"This is perfect!" exclaimed Bo appreciatively as she ran her hand along the benches and examined the neatly arranged kitchen implements. "My grandfather would have loved it here."

Mollie Green smiled. "All the comforts, more power than we can use, water as sweet as nectar. Bloody paradise. We want for nothing."

"We?" asked Bo. "You have family here?"

Mollie Green looked away. "You fancy a cuppatea, boys?" he asked, turning on a solar kettle and reaching for a battered old tin canister.

"So where is everyone?" asked Callum. He didn't like the way the old man had dodged Bo's question.

Mollie turned his back on them and started spooning brown, sticklike tea into the teapot.

"All gone now. My boys, they left, silly buggers. Thought they'd find themselves a girl out there somewhere. My brother went away, too. My wife . . . that was a long time ago. We came here to keep her safe. She died giving birth to our last boy. Saved her from the plague but I couldn't save her from Nature's revenge."

"But then why don't you shoot all the birds?" asked Bo.

"What for? There's no more womenfolk or baby girls to worry about. Without the birds, there'd be plagues of locusts, insects out of control."

"But there are still girls in other places. If you don't shoot the birds, they'll die," insisted Bo.

Mollie Green laughed. "You're a dreamer, just like my boy Ted. Thirty years ago, he went out searching, hoping to find a wife. Reckon he's searching still. But there are no more women out there. That's what we did to ourselves. You get used to it, sonny. You and that mate of yours, you can settle down together somewhere, hide away from the bad 'uns and the crazies. If you're rich enough, you can buy yourself a little boy out of a jam jar from that Colony mob. But you won't ever find yourself a wife. Those days are gone."

"I don't want a wife," said Bo. "I'm a—" she began.

Callum knew he had to stop her. "Shut up, Bo!"

"Oh, what!" said Bo, her hands on her hips. "You may think I'm peculiar, but it doesn't mean everyone in the world will."

"Keep it to yourself. You don't understand anything. You have to learn to keep your big mouth shut."

"Don't talk to me like that."

Mollie Green looked quizzically from Callum to Bo. "Now what's all the fuss?"

Before Callum could stop her, Bo turned to Mollie.

"I'm a girl. Callum thinks it's strange. He says I'm a freak."

Mollie Green didn't respond. He put one hand on the bench to steady himself. The color drained from his face and the tin canister fell from his hand to the floor, scattering black tea leaves across the dark, pressed earth.

"So you think that I'm a freak, too," said Bo. She turned to Callum, but he couldn't meet her gaze. He put his head in his hands and groaned.

Mollie stepped toward Bo and bent down so his face was level with hers. He was staring at her hard, as if he couldn't quite believe his eyes. Then he reached out and gently stroked her cheek.

"You sure?"

"Of course I'm sure. But I'm not going to prove it to you," said Bo.

Mollie Green pulled a chair out from the table and sat down heavily.

"No, you don't have to prove it to me. I believe you. Praise be, I believe in miracles."

15
Nature's Way

For the rest of the day, Mollie Green tiptoed around Bo as if she were made of glass. He took small notice of Callum. It made Callum feel he was nothing more than Bo's shadow.

Mollie insisted that the children stay in one of the empty bark huts, each with a room of their own. "You'll need to build your strength if you're going all the way to Vulture's Gate."

On the first night, Callum dragged the mattress from his bunk and into Bo's room. He set it down on the floor beside her bed and straightened out the worn blankets.

"I'll step on you if you put it there," said Bo.

"Maybe," answered Callum. "But you'll be safer."

"Safe from what?"

"Him," said Callum.

"You mean Mollie?" Bo laughed out loud. "He's not going to hurt us. I told you. He's like my Poppy, except he's shorter and rounder. He's not an Outstationer. We're not his prisoners. We can go any time we like."

"Tomorrow?" asked Callum.

"Maybe," said Bo evasively. "I need to sort out the problem with fuel and the Daisy-May. It may take a few days."

Callum didn't want to fight. He threw the blankets over his shoulder and lay down with his back to her.

In the morning, they woke to find a tray on the small table by the door of her room. There were two cups of warm tea, a slice of toasted seedbread smothered with honey, and a plate of sliced fruit.

Throughout the day, Mollie produced pieces of cake, slices of fruitbread, and other treats from his kitchen. When they weren't eating, he showed them all the technology that he used to farm the valley. Every time Callum tried to drag Bo away for a private conversation, Mollie would find another device to explain, another gadget with which to impress her.

First, it was the blanketing device he had designed that was automatically triggered whenever a scanner tried to read the terrain. Then they spent an hour comparing his Slugbot with Mr. Pinkwhistle. Callum tagged along while Mollie gave Bo a tour of his computer lab, where he had cobbled together working machines from a dozen forms of old technologies. He even showed them how he monitored the boundaries, explaining how he had seen Bo and Callum coming before they had crossed the rocky crest of hills.

The only moment of satisfaction Callum felt was when Mollie tried to take Bo into the aviary where he kept his sentry cockatoos. She stood behind Callum and refused to go near them. Finally, Mollie gave up and took the children into the kitchen where he laid out a platter of fresh fruit and poured them both a cup of strong black tea.

"Plenty of men still afraid of birds," he chuckled. "That's why I trained those fellas to attack."

"They don't scare me," said Callum.

"Shouldn't everyone be afraid of birds, especially me?" asked Bo.

"Lot of misunderstanding about the avian flu. It didn't pick favorites to begin with. Millions died and then, when they thought they had it under control, it mutated. That's when all the women and the little girls began to disappear. Even the women that survived, they lost the ability to bear girl children. My wife and me, we had five sons. Every time we conceived a baby girl, she miscarried. There's been two generations of boys with no sisters, men with no wives."

"But there's me. And I must have had a mother."

"Maybe womenfolk in your family developed a gene that's resistant to bird flu. Your grandfather probably took you into the bush to save you, Bo. He must have kept your mother and your grandmother in hiding, too. Women that could have babies were kidnapped, and if baby girls were born, they were taken away by the government, until the government fell to pieces."

"There's still the Colony government," said Callum.

"They're not a government," said Mollie scathingly. "They're a bunch of psychopathic wackos."

Callum slumped into angry silence. While Bo chatted with Mollie, Callum sat pensively beside her, looking out the window at the green hills and scuffing his bare feet on the pressed-earth floor. As the days slipped past, Callum spoke less and less.

One night, as they were returning to their hut after dinner, he grabbed Bo by the hand and gestured for her to follow him away from the central compound. He put his finger to his lips to indicate he needed her silence and led her into the orchard. When the lights of Mollie's hut were only a distant flicker, Callum turned to her.

"When are we going to leave?"

"What's the hurry? It's easy being here. We don't have to hide from Outstationers, there's plenty of food, and Mollie seems to like us."

"He likes *you*," said Callum. "Not me."

"But he's not mean to you," said Bo.

"I don't trust him. You know, he listens to us at night, when we're in our room. He has little devices all over the place. They don't work in the orchard because the cicadas drown them out. He watches every move we make and listens to every word we speak."

"He's taking care of us, Cal," said Bo, but her voice betrayed her uncertainty.

"You said you didn't need anyone to take care of you, and I don't want Mollie Green taking care of me. He's nothing to do with me. If we go to Vulture's Gate and find my dads, then we'll be with family."

"*Your* family," said Bo.

"They'll be yours, too. I've told you that before. Come

on, Bo. Every day that we spend with Mollie is another day away from my dads. I don't want them thinking I'm dead or lost forever."

Bo pulled up a blade of grass and chewed on the end of it, her brow furrowed with concentration.

"Soon," she said. "We'll go soon."

One afternoon, when they were near the end of their third week in the valley, Mollie Green started preparing dinner early. Callum stood by the window looking longingly at the distant horizon. Bo sat on a stool, picking luscious, ripe cherry tomatoes out of a bowl and watching as Mollie prepared all the different vegetables they'd harvested from his gardens.

Bo put her elbows on the table and rested her head in her hands, sighing with pleasure. "This is simply lovely," she said, as Mollie sliced a mango into a fan shape and arranged it on a platter.

"I felt like giving you kids a treat," said Mollie. "I'm making special things for both of you."

"I don't need anything special," said Callum.

Bo glared at him. "Don't mind Callum, Mollie," she said. "He's only a bit restless; he doesn't mean to be rude."

"Yes I do," said Callum. "Tell him, Bo. Tell him that we're leaving."

Bo twisted her hands in her lap and drew a deep breath. "You've been so good to us, Mollie, but Callum wants to go and find his dads. I think we might leave soon."

Mollie put his knife down. "Vulture's Gate is a dangerous place, Bo. Especially for you. Hell's Gate would be more fitting. As the women started to die off, the city tore itself apart. It's a cesspit of disease and unrest. You can't go there, Bo. It's not safe."

"But you said I wouldn't get sick. That I've probably got resistance to bird flu."

"There are worse things than disease in that city. The people, the men, they're sick at heart. It's not a safe place for a little girl."

"My fathers are there. Bo will be safe with them," interjected Callum.

"I'm not a little girl, Mollie, and I'm bigger than you, Callum. I'm almost a grown-up."

Mollie looked down and concentrated on slicing the vegetables. "I've got cooking to do. Dinner will be in half an hour. We'll talk about this later."

Callum and Bo walked down to the dam, in the heart of the valley, and spent an hour swimming in the warm, tea-brown water. Callum was almost too angry to talk to Bo. He floated on his back, staring at the high blue sky and wondering if he should run away by himself. By the time they returned to the kitchen, Mollie had changed his clothes and was setting the table.

"You look different," said Bo.

Mollie turned to face them, grinning. He was dressed in a dark blue suit and a checked gingham shirt.

"What's that thing you've got tied around your neck?" asked Callum.

"It's called a tie," said Mollie, flicking the piece of

brightly colored fabric out from inside his jacket. "Very old-fashioned but I like them. Folk used to wear 'em for special occasions. Pretty colors, eh?"

"But it's not a special occasion, is it?" asked Bo.

"Could be, could be," said Mollie, nodding seriously as he shook out a once-white but now yellowed tablecloth. Then he set his best, chipped white and gold crockery in place. Next, he positioned a battered silver candelabra in the middle of the table and jammed homemade candles into it. Bo and Callum sat opposite each other while Mollie straightened his tie and drew a deep breath, as if to make an announcement.

"I've been thinking about our conversation, thinking about what the future might hold for you kids." He looked Callum in the eye. "Boy, I know you want to go to Vulture's Gate and find your dads, but I've got another proposal for you. I've been thinking about it a lot these past few days and I want you to seriously consider what I'm about to offer."

Callum stared at Mollie warily.

"So, what I was thinking, boy, is, if you give me a chance, I could be a father to you. Teach you 'bout permaculture. How to make this place work, how to take care of yourself and Bo."

For a moment, Callum softened toward the old man. "Thanks, Mollie. But I've already got a father. Two fathers. I don't need another one."

"You're not listening to me. I can offer you a safe home. Not something you'll find in Vulture's Gate. You can't take that girl there. She needs looking after."

"Mollie, I do not need looking after," said Bo.

"Now I know you're a proud young missy," said Mollie. "And that's something I like about you. My own mother and my wife were proud women. It's a lovely thing in a gal. Which is why I've got something to propose to you, too, Bo. Something important."

Clumsily, Mollie stretched across the table and took Bo's hand. He held it tightly as he began to speak, though he kept his eyes closed, as if what he was saying required every ounce of his concentration.

"I know I'm an old coot and you're still a strip of a girl. But in a year or less, you'll start changing, filling out, turning into a woman."

Bo tried to pull her hand free but Mollie wouldn't let go. He looked up at her now, his blue eyes watery, his gaze determined.

"A woman is better off having a man to protect her, Bo. Be a long while before Callum is a real man. So you and me, we should get married. I'll treat you right, take care of you. You'll be safe here with me. That's what a husband is for—to safekeep his wife. I'll husband you, be a father to Callum and then, when my time is over, Callum will still be young enough to take my place. Be your husband in my stead. Maybe follow on as a father to those sons you and I will make together one day."

Bo wrenched her hand free and jumped up from the table, catching the tablecloth by its edge and bringing all the crockery to the floor with a crash. "I don't want to be your wife!" she shouted.

"You're crazy, old man," yelled Callum, kicking his

chair aside and snatching a knife from the scattered cutlery. Brandishing the weapon, Callum backed away from the table with Bo beside him. But Mollie moved quickly, stepping between them and the doorway, slamming the door shut and barring their escape.

"Nature's way, kiddies. This is Nature's way. The ancients, they gave the young girls to the old men, 'cause they were the ones that knew how to care for them. I can help you both. Save you. It's only natural that you should be my wife, Bo."

"Keep away from her, you crazy old man," shouted Callum.

"Listen here, runt . . ." said Mollie, knocking the knife from Callum's hand and twisting his arm behind his back.

Bo stuck both her fingers in her ears and shut her eyes. "Stop it! *Stop it!*" she cried, her voice a piercing wail of misery.

In the silence that followed, they heard Mr. Pinkwhistle at the door, scrabbling at the timber.

Mollie released Callum, as if he'd finally realized the full import of what had happened.

"Settle down, settle down," he muttered, raising his two hands in the air in a sign of surrender. "No need to make a decision right away. Plenty of time. You two have a think about everything I've proposed and we'll talk about it in the morning."

Back in their hut, Callum turned on Bo. "See, I told you. Tomorrow, we're out of here."

Bo nodded but she lay down on her bed and covered

her face with her arms. That's when they heard the bolt slide across.

Callum ran to the door and tried to push it open but it was secured on the outside.

"Hey," he yelled, pounding on the wood with his fists. "What do you think you're doing?"

"Keeping you safe," yelled Mollie Green. Callum raced to the window and watched in disbelief as Mollie fixed a sheet of black metal against the glass. Then he circled the hut, hammering covers over every possible exit, sealing the two children inside.

16
Fitcher's Birds

"Great," said Callum. "Now we're trapped."

"He can't mean to hurt us," said Bo.

"Didn't you hear what he said? He wants you to be his wife! He's the bad guy, Bo. Like in those stories you told me about Bluebeard and Fitcher. He wants to keep you forever."

Callum threw himself down beside Bo and pressed his face against the pillow.

"*Fitcher's Bird*," said Bo thoughtfully.

She put one arm across Callum and whispered in his ear.

"In *Fitcher's Bird*, the girl runs away. Remember? She tricks the old wizard by rolling in honey and then covering herself with feathers so he passes her on the road and doesn't recognize her."

Callum turned to face her. They were so close he could

feel her breath against his cheek. He nuzzled his mouth close to her ear in case Mollie was listening to their conversation.

"I don't think honey and feathers will work, but we could still run away," he whispered. "You know we have to run away, don't you?"

Bo nodded and Callum felt a flood of relief rush through him. The last few days, when he had toyed with the idea of running away alone, of getting to Vulture's Gate by himself without Bo's help, had left him feeling cold and lonely. Now, everything had shifted again. Bo wanted to be with him.

"We need to think of a plan," she whispered.

At that moment, Callum couldn't think of anything but how good it felt to be close to Bo again. In the desert they had slept side by side, but since arriving in the valley Callum had stayed on his mattress on the floor. He realized how much he'd missed lying close to her. He shut his eyes and rested his forehead against her neck. Her long hair tickled his cheek but he didn't mind. He simply wanted to breathe in the smell of her for a little longer.

Callum woke with a start. Mollie was dragging him off the bed and across the floor.

"Fine kettle of fish!" he shouted. "Finding you two in bed together. Should never have started that conversation with you around, boy. Should have known it would give you ideas."

"What?" yelled Callum, trying to shake himself free of Mollie's iron grip.

"Mollie!" shouted Bo. "What are you doing? You're hurting him."

But Mollie slammed the door shut in Bo's face.

Callum kicked and screamed as Mollie twisted his wrists and dragged him across the compound to the edge of the circle of huts. He wrenched open the door of the cockatoo aviary and threw Callum inside.

"You need to think about what it means to betray your father. You can spend tonight in here. Tomorrow, I'll fix up another hut," said Mollie gruffly as he chained the aviary door shut. "No more of this two-in-a-bed business. It's time we got serious about our future, son."

"I'm not your son!" shouted Callum. "I don't want a future with you!"

Above him, the cockatoos squawked and fluttered on their perches. Callum covered his head with his hands, waiting for them to attack. When he looked up, Mollie was gone and the birds were settling down, their sulphur crests flat and their eyes blinking sleepily. He wrapped his arms around himself and sank lower into the mess of bird droppings on the aviary floor as the moon crept up over the valley.

Hours later Callum lay crumpled in the corner of the aviary, trying to sleep, when he saw a ripple of movement in the shadows across the yard. For a moment he thought it was a wild animal, but when it crossed into a patch of moonlight he realized it was Mr. Pinkwhistle. The robo-raptor moved swiftly along the edge of the buildings, circling the yard, keeping in the shadows until he reached the aviary.

"Hey, Mr. Pinkwhistle," whispered Callum. For the first time, he was glad to see the roboraptor staring at him with beady red eyes.

Mr. Pinkwhistle bobbed his head and then lunged forward, snapping his jaw shut on a mouthful of wire. Callum managed to get his fingers out of the way just in time. Mr. Pinkwhistle's teeth tore through the mesh as if it was fairy floss. In less than a minute, he'd gouged a hole in the cage big enough for Callum to climb through. He scurried along the edge of the buildings in the shadows and Callum followed. When they reached the door of Bo's hut, he was relieved to find it was simply bolted. He unlocked the door as quietly as he could and pushed it open.

He was about to whisper Bo's name when a hand slid across his face, clamping his mouth shut. He nodded to signal he understood. Moving as quickly and quietly as possible, they hurried into the orchards. It was only when they were in the dappled moonlight among the trees that Callum realized what Bo had done.

"Your hair," he said. "What did you do to your hair?"

Bo raised one hand to the bare skin on the nape of her neck. "I cut it off and spread it across my pillow. I used your bedding to shape a body under my blankets and then I gave it my hair."

Callum stared at her. She looked much younger without her long dark mane. She had hacked her hair off unevenly and jagged tendrils framed her face. He touched her cheek.

"Why?" he said.

"Because Mollie came back to my hut after he locked you in the aviary."

"Did he hurt you?"

"No. He told me what he'd done with you and said we all needed to work out how to live together. We talked for a long time and I asked him all about the cameras and how he watches us."

"And he turned them off?"

"No," said Bo. "But I found out he doesn't record anything, so he has to be watching us to see what's going on. After he locked me in I took Mr. Pinkwhistle under the covers with me and watched his sensors. I could tell when Mollie had gone to bed so I knew he wasn't watching me. Then I hacked off my hair and spread it across the pillow. If Mollie does look, he'll think I'm asleep."

"But how did Mr. Pinkwhistle get out?"

"Up the stovepipe of the old woodstove. He fit perfectly."

"Mollie will see I've escaped," said Callum. "It won't take him long to figure that out. He knows where the Daisy-May is, too. He'll follow us."

"Not until dawn." She took Callum's hand and they ran through the night orchard. Mr. Pinkwhistle loped ahead of them, his head swiveling back to check that they were keeping up.

They avoided the main pathways, weaving their way through the vineyards and orchards, past the dam and the water tanks until they reached the thick stands of bamboo. They had nearly beaten their way through the dense foliage that rose like a black wall on either side of them when they heard cockatoos screeching. Above them, the sky was tinged with dawn light. Bo stopped in her tracks and looked around for somewhere to hide, her eyes wide with terror.

"We can't outrun them," she said. "And they'll have woken Mollie."

"Don't stop," said Callum, dragging her in his wake, forcing her to keep moving.

Minutes later, the first cockatoo attacked, tearing out a handful of Callum's hair, while the others circled above, signaling to Mollie the location of the runaways. Bo fell back into a stand of bamboo, trying to bend the long green stalks over her body for protection while Mr. Pinkwhistle lunged at the air, snapping at the birds.

"*Fitcher's Bird*," muttered Callum, suddenly realizing what he had to do. Next time the biggest cockatoo swooped over him, he snatched at its feet and wings, dragging it to the ground. It flapped and shrieked but Callum kept it pinned down.

"Bo, quick, give me your jacket," he called.

Bo crawled out of the bamboo. She was shivering as she knelt down in the dirt and stripped off her catskin coat. Callum covered the bird and it immediately stopped struggling. Then he gestured for Bo to help.

"Hold him down."

"I can't," said Bo, backing away.

"You have to—just for a minute—while I do something," he shouted above the screeches of the birds. He forced her hands onto the jacket, pinning down the cockatoo.

The other birds continued to dive-bomb while Callum tore his shirt into strips and swiftly knotted a makeshift rope.

"Okay, this is what we're going to do. I'm going to tie this cocky to Mr. Pinkwhistle," he said, fastening a loop of cloth to the bird's leg, while still keeping its head covered. "You need to program him to run around the top of the valley, in the opposite direction to us. If you can program him to lead the cockies away, to give us time to reach the Daisy-May, then Mr. P can bite through the rope and run across the hilltop to meet us. It might buy us just enough time."

Bo nodded and drew Mr. Pinkwhistle onto her lap. She sat with the roboraptor draped across her knees, his chest open, her face a study in fierce concentration as she punched in coordinates and directions.

As soon as Mr. Pinkwhistle was on his feet, Callum uncovered the tethered cockatoo. Immediately, the rest of the flock gave up on the children. They followed the struggling, captive leader north, squawking and shrieking above him and the roboraptor.

Callum only glanced over his shoulder once as they headed into the bamboo. Far away, flapping frantically above the hillside path, the flock of cockatoos circled and dove at Mr. Pinkwhistle as he led them farther and farther away from the two children.

They had been running for hours by the time they crested the rise and found the Daisy-May.

"We probably still don't have enough fuel to reach Vulture's Gate," said Bo. "I only half-filled her tanks."

"Don't worry," said Callum. "Early yesterday morning, while you and Mollie were still asleep, I topped them up. I've even filled the reserves and stuffed one of the panniers with pineapples. I figure they should work as well as cactus."

Bo looked at him in surprise and then grinned. "Even if you're a boy, you're as cunning as Fitcher's bird!"

They rode down through the thick scrub and turned along a worn trail at the base of the hillside. Suddenly Bo braked and turned her eyes to the hills. Callum watched, too, waiting. They both laughed with relief as Mr. Pinkwhistle came charging out of the scrub. Bo swept him into her arms and set him on the tank before her.

Toward midday, they pulled off the road and drove down a dirt track to find a sheltered place to rest. Bo opened the saddlebag to search for their sleeping kit.

"Did you put these in here?" she asked. Callum stood beside her and stared into the pannier. Neatly stacked inside were all Bo's weapons, her string carrier of hunting tools, and a brown paper bag. Tied on with coarse twine was a note in wobbly handwriting:

Sometimes old men dream foolish dreams. Travel safe—Mollison Green.

"He knew we were going to run away," said Bo, as she opened the paper bag and looked in at the ripening tomatoes and bananas.

"He was crazy," said Callum.

"But he was sad and lonely, too," said Bo. "All those long nights listening to the sound of your own breathing, with no other living soul to care if you never woke up again."

"Don't feel too sorry for him," said Callum. "He would have had you bringing up babies like he does tomatoes. They'd be springing out of your mouth before you knew what hit you."

Bo laughed. "Babies don't come out of people's mouths!"

"So where do you think they come from—when they don't come from clinics? How do they get from the inside out?"

Bo blushed. "I haven't spent much time thinking about it. I suppose they come out the same way baby animals do—between the legs."

They both fell quiet, trapped in the awkwardness of the moment. "Well, no wonder girls are extinct," said Callum.

17
Gateway to the Underworld

Callum had to fight down his impatience as the city of Vulture's Gate loomed on the horizon. They'd been traveling for days on end, making few stops, and both their food and fuel supplies were low. Now that he knew they were in the homestretch, he wanted to be there instantly. He couldn't wait to be inside the old apartment in the heart of the city and finally in the arms of his fathers. He played it over and over again in his mind, that moment when he would step over the threshold and they would embrace him. Yet he knew Bo was right when she insisted they set up camp in the mountains south of the city.

"I think it would be better to arrive in daylight. We can leave at first light and be there by early morning. If this place is as awful as Mollie Green said, we want to be able to see our way around."

"It's not that bad. Mollie was trying to scare you. Once we reach my dads, everything will be fine," said Callum. He pointed at the tiny glow of distant lights. "That bright bit, that's the Colony on South Head. Most Colony people lived there but we lived in this really cool apartment building outside the wall. It has a lot of security around it, so once we get inside we'll be safe. It's only the streets that are dangerous."

"And are there vultures?" asked Bo anxiously.

"I don't think so. I don't even know what a vulture looks like."

Bo knelt down beside him and drew a small sketch in the dirt. "Poppy read me stories about vultures. He said a goddess with a vulture's head guarded the gateway to the underworld."

Callum looked at the symbol of the vulture and kicked dust across it. "You know too many stories," he said, trying to make his voice sound cheerful.

Mr. Pinkwhistle brought them a possum, and Bo threw the carcass onto their small fire. The air filled with the smell of scorched fur. When it was cooked, she cut away the charred skin and sliced thick pieces of meat for Callum and herself.

"I miss Mollie's food," said Bo.

"I don't," said Callum, chewing grimly on his slice of possum meat. "You wait. My dads will make sure we have plenty to eat. Maybe they'll build another Refuge somewhere safer and we'll go live there. Or maybe we'll live in the apartment."

"What if they don't want me?"

"I've told you. They'll be fine. They might be a bit freaked out by you being a girl. But they'll get used to it. As long as you don't turn into a woman, it will all be okay."

"But I will turn into a woman, Callum." She opened her shirt and looked down at her bare chest. "Sometimes my nipples tingle and they've changed shape. Only a little bit. But they're not smooth and flat anymore. They have little pointy tips, see?"

Callum looked away. "Close your shirt," he snapped.

"What's the matter?"

"There's nothing the matter with me. I'm normal."

Bo snorted. She crawled around the campfire and knelt in front of him. "Look at you. You're scruffy and dirty and covered in scars. How can you tell me what to do when you don't even know how to tie your own shirt?"

Callum let her straighten the stays of the old catskin shirt she had given him. She ran her fingers through his hair, combing it away from his face. It had grown so long that it brushed against his shoulders.

"Bo," he said, taking her face in his hands and drawing it close. "Whatever happens tomorrow, you know that you're my best friend. My best friend in the world." He put his face next to hers and swept his eyelashes against her cheek in a butterfly kiss.

As the embers of the fire grew low, Bo drew him down to lie beside her. He curled against the warm curve of her body, savoring the comfort of her arms. Tomorrow everything would be different. He tried not to think about what that would mean.

*   *   *

As they approached the city, Callum could feel tension mounting in Bo's body. She leaned close to the bike and focused on the road to avoid driving into one of the gaping craters that pockmarked the highway. Burned-out vehicles littered the shoulder. Drifts of burning rubble glowed orange through a smoldering haze. A shadowy figure emerged from the smoke and then disappeared, as if it were an apparition.

"Has there been a war?" asked Bo.

"I don't know. There have always been crazy outsiders attacking the Colony. But I don't remember any of this."

No wonder his fathers had wanted to take him away. He couldn't recall ever seeing this devastation when they'd lived in Vulture's Gate but was that because his fathers always kept him cocooned inside their apartment? He had been so small when they left the city that all his memories were surrounded by a soft infant glow.

They passed hundreds of abandoned buildings. Some were overgrown with vines, others had trees growing out through cavernous black windows. A murder of crows flew cawing through the broken roof of a bombed house. Bo slowed the Daisy-May as the highway disappeared beneath a swampy mass of refuse and sludge. They traveled for miles without seeing anyone until a ragged man, almost naked except for a cloth around his waist, stumbled across the road and vanished into a crater. Callum shifted uncomfortably in his seat and Bo reached back, squeezing his knee to make him stop wriggling.

The Nehkbet Tower was easy to navigate toward, dark and solid above the ruined city. Its black glass walls rose up like the barrel of a gun, pointing straight into a hazy blue sky.

"It doesn't look like a homey sort of place," said Bo.

"Don't let that or the security put you off. Once we're inside, everything will be great. But there are checkpoints to get through before we're safe. The first test will be the security drone at the gateway," he said nervously.

But as they drew closer to the black gates they could see that the entrance to the Nehkbet Tower courtyard was a bomb site. One of the gates lay twisted and torn from its hinges, jutting out of a crater.

"What should I do?" asked Bo.

"Don't stop," said Callum. "Skirt around it and take us straight to the main doors."

Bo revved the Daisy-May and drove straight up the steps of the building and along the colonnaded entrance. She braked only when they were close to the vaultlike front doors.

"Home time!" said Callum. Bo pressed the release and the protective shield of the Daisy-May slid back. They were hit by a wave of sticky, humid air. "We have to be fast. Once Ruff and Rusty know I'm here everything will be fine, but we don't want anyone mistaking us for Festers."

"Festers?"

"Don't worry." Callum grabbed her hand and dragged her off Daisy-May.

Bo set Mr. Pinkwhistle on guard while they turned their attention to the access boxes on the south wall. Callum counted his way past the blank screens until he reached Box 217. When he found it, he was almost too excited to speak. He pushed his hand against the imprint bar and his face against the retinal scanner and waited for the screen to light up. "I have to still be in the system! I have to," he muttered. He gave a shout of relief when Ruff and Rusty's faces appeared on the access screen.

"Dads, it's me!" he said. "Let me in!" But the faces staring back at him smiled blankly and intoned, "You have activated Ruff and Rusty's message box. Please say your piece and we'll get back to you."

"Why aren't they answering you?" asked Bo.

"Maybe they're asleep. Or they might be out. I hope not. I can get into the building but if someone spots me looking like this and with no microchips in my ears, I could be in trouble."

Bo glanced over her shoulder anxiously, scanning the arcade.

"Should we wait somewhere else until they come back? My 'twition says this is a bad place to be," she said, pointing up at the surveillance cameras monitoring the arcade.

"Don't rush me. I want to leave a proper message first." Callum turned back to the message bank. "I'm safe. I'm going to try coming up but if someone stops me, at least you know I'm here in Vulture's Gate. And I've got this friend with me and you're really going to like . . . them." He was suddenly uncertain about calling Bo a "she." It seemed rude.

At the entrance to the Tower, there was another retinal scanner. Callum turned to Bo and put his hands on her shoulders.

"You wait here," he said. "You can't come into the building unless you're in the system. I'll talk to someone and sort everything out. Stay with the Daisy-May. I won't be long. I'll come back for you," he said.

Inside, the white and silver foyer was empty. Callum was relieved to see it looked the same as he remembered. But where were the Squadrones that guarded the place? Where was the Colony drone who usually manned the front desk? Callum caught sight of his reflection in the polished metal of the elevator doors. He looked like a runaway. He touched his scarred ears anxiously. Would a drone believe he had once been a Colony boy? He could hardly believe it himself.

No one stopped the elevator as it rose up through the building. On the seventeenth floor, Callum made his way to the old apartment, down long, silent corridors. It was eerie how empty the building appeared. Nervously, he pressed his hand against the apartment's imprint sensor. What if the scars on his hands interfered with the reading? When the panel failed to acknowledge him, he leaned his head against the smooth, shiny door and sighed. This wasn't the homecoming he'd dreamed of. A single tear ran down his cheek. "Dads," he whispered.

As if the apartment itself heard him, the door swung open. Inside, nothing was as he remembered it. The place was a mess. There were piles of dirty dishes on every surface, and the air smelled stale. Drawers had been pulled open, and sheets of paper were scattered across the floor. Callum picked up a small square of stationery with a black flower in the middle. There were no words on the page, only neat ebony petals fanning out from the center of the white sheet.

"You, Fester! How did you get in here?" yelled a voice.

Callum jumped. A gray-haired man stood in the doorway of the apartment, blocking Callum's exit.

"I'm Callum Caravaggio. I'm looking for my fathers."

"There are no Caravaggios here."

"Where has everyone gone?"

"Anyone with brains or luck is living on South Head." The man walked toward Callum, as if approaching a wild dog. "You can't be a Caravaggio."

Callum backed away until he was pressed against the window. Down in the Tower courtyard the Daisy-May was waiting for him, but it was no longer parked discreetly. It was speeding around the edge of the building with a Pally-val hovering in pursuit.

"Bo!" he cried.

Before the gray-haired man could stop him, Callum dived past, skidding over the scattered paper, slamming the apartment door shut behind him, and dashing down the hallway. He could hear the man chasing him but he didn't stop. He swung into the elevator and hit the ground-floor button.

When he stepped outside again, a pair of drones on a Pally-val were hurtling down the arcade toward him. Callum zigzagged between the colonnades, making it impossible for the drones to take a clear shot at him.

Suddenly the Daisy-May came roaring around the corner of the building and the shield slid back.

"Quick, Callum," called Bo as she slowed near him. "Jump."

Callum didn't need to be told twice. As the bike glided past him, he mustered all his circus training. He took a running leap and flung himself into the air, landing neatly on the slow-moving vehicle. The shield of the Daisy-May was barely closed when the guards opened fire again. Bo revved the engine and the bike leaped off the top of the steps. Callum felt his bones jar as it landed in the street. He could see the muscles and sinews in Bo's arms quivering as she tried to keep control.

"Where can we hide?" shouted Bo.

"Just drive," said Callum. Why hadn't he anticipated this and made a backup plan? The Daisy-May sped out of the central area and into the cluttered streets of the city's dark side. It fishtailed wildly as Bo gunned the accelerator. Out of nowhere, a monster truck pulled in front of them and before she could steady it the Daisy-May was on its side, careering down a narrow city street. Mr. Pinkwhistle let out a long, shrill cry. As soon as the bike came to a stop, Bo tried to make the shield peel back but it was jammed shut. For a moment, Callum had a horrible vision of the patrols smashing the blue glass, dragging them out, and shooting them both before they could explain. Bo screamed at him to cover his eyes as she set Mr. Pinkwhistle against the shield. The roboraptor sat back on his haunches and then launched himself against the cover, blasting a hole through it that generated a shower of tiny dark shards. Callum shook the glass from his hair and looked out into the street.

There was noise everywhere—sirens, shouting, and the sound of jackbooted feet racing toward them. Bo and Callum crawled out of the wreckage of the Daisy-May and ran. Bo grabbed the handrail at the top of a long, slimy flight of stairs that disappeared beneath the city, and started descending into the dark.

"Stop, wait," called Callum. "We can't go down there."

"There are people chasing us," said Bo. "People with weapons."

"That's an old underground train station. They're all flooded. I've heard about them. We go down there, we'll drown in the darkness."

"There's a muon detector in Mr. Pinkwhistle. He'll help us find our way."

"Maybe we should put our hands up and surrender. Then they can take us to my dads. They'll know I'm on the register."

"But I'm not," said Bo. "What if they won't listen to you?"

Callum bit his lip. His dads had always warned him against being found alone, being mistaken for a runaway or a reject. If it was dangerous for him, how would a girl be treated?

The sirens grew louder and still Callum stood transfixed, staring into the darkness.

"Callum?"

Bo gazed up at him, waiting. Callum followed her down into the fetid dark.

18
Black Water

For one long and terrible moment, Bo had thought Callum was going to leave her. She had seen it written on his face when he stood at the top of the stairs—that split second of hesitation as he contemplated whether to follow her into the darkness. As they hurried into the underground, she reached for his hand.

Black water washed around their ankles. Shadows fell like dark wings as they descended the steps and walked along a tunnel. Once they were below the streets, slivers of light pierced through cracks above them. Soon the darkness thickened to soupy blackness. Bo stroked Mr. Pinkwhistle until his eyes shone with thin, bright LED lights that cast a pale glow before them. As the tunnel started to dip downward, the water grew deeper. Bo tied her string bag into a bundle to carry on her head.

"This water is stinky," said Callum. "I think I'd rather be pulverized by the Squadrones than drown in a sewer."

Bo hooked one arm around Callum's shoulder and drew him close. "Be very still and listen."

They stood side by side, concentrating, craning their ears into the black air. At first, all that was audible was the sound of dripping water. Then she heard it again. Something was slapping against the surface of the floodwater.

"It's coming this way," said Bo.

She turned off the lights in Mr. Pinkwhistle and the darkness pressed in around them. A moment later, she could sense something nearby. Something big—a boat or canoe.

"Coo-eee?" came a voice, not much more than a whisper but soft and shrill.

Bo held her breath.

"You Fester or foe?" came the whisper again. "You be Fester, you be safe," it said in a wheedling tone. It was not until the sound of the slapping oars faded into the distance that Bo felt she could breathe again.

"Maybe they could have helped us," said Bo, though even as she spoke, she doubted that anyone in Vulture's Gate could help them. Not even Callum's fathers.

"C'mon," said Callum, "we're going aboveground. There's nowhere safe down here, and my feet are getting soggy. Besides, it creeps me out, this dark."

Bo grabbed his arm and held him back. She flicked open Mr. Pinkwhistle's chest.

"Look," she said, pulling him over to stare at the tiny

screen. "See this green light? That's muons. It means there are spaces down here."

"Yeah," grumbled Callum. "Spaces full of water. We can't go any farther."

Bo ignored him. She peered closely at the grid on Mr. Pinkwhistle's screen.

"Off to the right, there's some big, open place, like a cave. There's a little narrow tunnel that leads into it—a pathway we can follow. It might be a good place to hide for the night."

"I hate the dark," said Callum.

"It's comforting. It feels like the burrow," said Bo.

Before Callum could stop her, she started wading through the water with Mr. Pinkwhistle held high above her head, feeling her way along the slimy wall, looking for the narrow path that the roboraptor's sensors had displayed.

From above, they could still hear the wail of sirens out on the street. And faintly, an echo bouncing across the dark water, came the eerie voices calling "Coo-ee." They were so deep into the tunnel now that all that was visible was the glow of Mr. Pinkwhistle's eyes. Small pinpricks of red light glanced off every surface.

The water grew deeper until it was washing around their chests. The air was fetid, and it felt as though there was little oxygen left in it. Bo tried not to breathe too deeply. Then she felt Callum tugging at her belt. "Let's turn back, Bo. This feels wrong."

"Listen," she said. From some way ahead of them, they could hear the sound of falling water.

"So?"

"So it means there's a cavern ahead. We'll be safe there. I know we will. My 'twition tells me."

"Bo," he said, the single word an admonition. She was glad she couldn't see him rolling his eyes in the gloomy darkness.

"Just a little farther," she said. "Trust me."

The water grew shallower and began to move faster, rushing around their knees so that they had trouble keeping their balance. And then they were at the lip of the waterfall, looking into a cavern.

"See," said Bo. They knelt at the entrance and stared in amazement. A black pool lay thirty feet below them, lit from above by a soft, greenish light. The air smelled different here, sharp and salty, and down by the water there was a metal dock.

"This place is humongous," said Callum, peering into the gloom.

Bo leaned into the cavern, checking for a way down. Beneath them, the wall was covered with rickety, tiered platforms. Mr. Pinkwhistle let out a husky growl as Bo slipped over the edge of the tunnel and onto a platform a few feet below. It shuddered as she landed.

"C'mon," she called. "It's safe."

The platform was three feet wide and was edged with a rusty metal railing. Bo watched as Callum shut his eyes and jumped, landing sure-footed as a cat on the narrow shelf.

"You're crazy," she said, as she steadied him with one hand.

"Me?"

"Yes. You. Why did you shut your eyes? You couldn't see where you were going to land."

Callum grinned. "You've got your 'twition. I've got my instinct. I didn't spend all that time being tossed around like a beanbag for nothing. Sometimes it's best to let your body take you. Besides, I figured you'd catch me if I missed."

Bo shook her head but she couldn't help smiling. How could she have imagined he would abandon her? They edged their way along the platform. The tiers followed a zigzag pattern around the walls. Each time they jumped from one platform to another beneath, Bo felt her head spin. By the time they were halfway down the walls, she was giddy and breathless.

"Can we stop for a rest?" she said, sitting down on the platform and putting one hand to her forehead.

"Are you all right?" asked Callum, kneeling down beside her and gazing into her face.

"Not really. But you look strange, too," she said.

"My legs feel itchy," he said. He rolled up the leg of his trousers and screamed. Black, slimy slugs clung to every inch of his skin. He jumped to his feet and tore off his shirt.

"My back, my back, they're on my back, too!" His shouts reverberated around the cavern.

Bo slapped at the leeches, trying to knock them away, but they clung fast.

"No," screamed Callum. "Don't pull them out. They poison you if you rip them off."

"What are they?"

"Leeches," said Callum faintly.

Bo lifted her shirt and looked down at her belly. She was covered in them, too. She let out a soft whistle of astonishment and Mr. Pinkwhistle tipped his head to one side, listening with curiosity.

As Bo and Callum stood staring at the hundreds of leeches covering their bodies, the black pond beneath them began to bubble and froth. A battered black and gray machine rose up out of the depths and clanked against the side of the dock. Before Callum and Bo could decide what it was, a horde of boys emerged from a hatch on top of the machine. They scurried up the platforms, leaping across the railings like a tribe of monkeys. In an instant, they surrounded Bo and Callum.

"Festers," hissed Callum.

19
The Festers

Two small, skinny boys swung onto the platform behind them and blocked any chance Bo and Callum had of retreating into the tunnel. Others crowded around, studying them closely. One boy, tall and powerfully built, pushed his way to the front of the pack. He wore a tight-fitting beanie, from beneath which bright white tufts of hair stuck out. He leaned in close to Bo and grabbed her by the front of her shirt. From under her arm, Mr. Pinkwhistle growled, then he clamped his jaws around the boy's wrist and held it fast.

"No, Mr. Pinkwhistle," said Bo, slipping a finger into the roboraptor's jaw and triggering the release.

"Mr. Pinkwhistle?" The boy held his bruised wrist and his eyes grew narrow. "I want him. He's better than a dog."

"You can't have him. He's mine."

"Everything down here is mine."

"Not us and not Mr. Pinkwhistle," said Bo firmly.

"What are you doing in our dock?" said the boy. "You escape from somewhere?"

"We were being chased. This seemed safe."

"Safe for us, not for you," said the boy. His gang laughed and one of them shoved Callum, trying to throw him off balance.

Callum stood as straight as he could, wishing he could make himself taller. "You don't own this place," he said. "You're not the boss of the world."

"I'm the boss of *this* world," said the boy.

"Let's push 'em off. Let's 'bort 'em," said the small boy who had shoved Callum.

"Shut up, Flakie," said the boss.

"Who are you?" asked Bo.

"I'm Roc," he said. "And these are my Diseases." He gestured to the crowd of boys.

"You mean you're all Festers," muttered Callum.

"What?" said Bo, looking from Roc to Callum.

"Festers," said Callum. "These guys are Festers. They feed off garbage and they eat dead people."

"We do not," said Flakie, making as if to shove Callum again. Roc pulled him back, then spoke directly to Bo. "That's a stupid story that men tell their children to make us sound scary. We're the new bogey-boys."

"You don't look very scary," said Bo.

"I *am* scary," said Roc.

"Not to me," said Bo.

Roc looked Bo up and down appraisingly. "You're

either brave or reckless or maybe stupid. It won't take me long to figure out which."

"We won't be here long enough for that. We'll go back up through the tunnels soon. When it's dark."

"It's not safe up there after dark. You're better off down here."

"Not with these things feeding on us." Bo lifted up her shirt and showed her belly where the leeches were growing plump with blood.

Roc smiled.

"Flakie and Blister will take them off you. They're old hands at it," said Roc. "You wait here with them. The Diseases and I have work to do. You and me, we'll talk more when I've finished my business."

Before they could answer, Roc and his tribe had swarmed past them, up the rails to the tunnel. The two small boys stayed behind.

"Here, Roc says we have to clean youse up," said one of them.

"Don't touch me," said Callum, pushing their clawing hands away from him. "We can't stay here, Bo. We need to find my dads."

"First, we need to get rid of these leeches," she said. She turned to the two Festers. "Show me how you do it. Show me how you get these things off."

"You go for the little suckers," said Flakie. "If you try and rip 'em off, they spit garbage and leave their tails inside you. Then you get all scabby and sick, like."

"I remember that," said Callum. "I had one on my leg when I was a kid."

"One? That all? I've been flicking these off boys for years," said Blister. "Millions of 'em."

Blister bent forward and placed a sharp, dirty fingernail on Bo's belly beside one of the leeches. When the small sucker was loosened, he flicked at its ripe body with his other hand while he used his fingernail to detach the second sucker. Then with one swift movement he swept it over the edge of the platform.

"Now, that was just to show you how youse do it. Take your duds off and I'll clear the rest of them."

Moving slowly, Bo took off her shirt and turned around so Blister could see the leeches clustered on her lower back. "You do the ones I can't reach. I'll do my front," she said.

Sighing, Callum followed suit, stripping off his shirt so Flakie could clear his torso. The boys worked quickly, deftly, until Bo and Callum's chests ran with little trails of blood from where the leeches had been removed.

"They spit this stuff in you, makes your blood go thin. It's not bad stuff. Not like poison or garbage. Long as you take 'em off proper, they won't make you sick. You won't bleed long neither. We get them all out clean and you'll heal up real quick. You better take your pants off," said Blister matter-of-factly.

Callum looked across at Bo, panic-stricken. Bo nodded to reassure him. There would be a lot of uncomfortable questions if she took off her trousers.

"I've figured it out now," she told Blister. "I can take the rest of them off myself. Callum has more of them. Go on, Callum. Take your trousers off. Blister can help Flakie and you'll be cleaned up faster."

Blister shrugged and turned to watch Callum remove his trousers. While the two Festers cleared the last of the leeches from Callum's body, Bo pulled out the waist of her pants and checked her crotch.

When they had finished, Flakie and Blister led Bo and Callum down to where the battered submarine was moored at the dock beneath. They stood by the water's edge, throwing pebbles into the pool, waiting for the return of Roc and the rest of the gang.

"How far have you come in this machine?" asked Bo, admiring the sub.

"North Shore. We take the harbor tunnel. No mines down there like there is in the open water, so we can scoot across real fast. No one else is game to use it. Bits of it collapse all the time. But nothing scares Roc."

"'Cause he's too stupid to be frightened," muttered Callum.

"What?" said Blister, shoving Callum roughly.

Bo stepped between them. "He does sound brave. What did Roc mean when he said you all had a job to do?"

"Raids."

As Blister spoke, from far away they heard a distant booming.

"That's them," said Flakie. "They just blew up today's target."

"Blew it up?"

"Yeah," said Blister, picking at a scab on his knee. "That's what we do. We blow up the olds. Make it better for kids and all."

"You *what*?" said Callum.

"Blow up the olds. All the mobs that hurt us kids. You know, if they catch you, they lock you up in the factories. That's where the boys get put when they're caught. Or they make you slaves and lackeys. So we blow them up."

"But what about the boys in the factories?"

"We make sure they can run free. If they make it to the North Shore, Roc lets them join us. And sometimes he still rescues the littlies, too. Fishes them out of dumpsters. That's where me and Flakie came from. That's how Roc started. He started fishing for the littlies and then, as we got bigger, he started making us his gang and doing the raids."

"They're on a big job today. Gonna blow up the Nehkbet Tower. Roc reckons that will really do the oldies' heads in." Blister giggled and Flakie joined in.

"Not the Tower!" cried Callum.

"What's wrong with you? You on their side?" said Blister, his eyes narrowing.

Bo put her arm around Callum. "When will Roc be back?"

"Not for a while," said Flakie. "Last time they blew the gates, this time they're going for the forecourt. Next time they'll bring the whole wasps' nest down."

Bo turned to Callum, registering his rising panic. "It

will be all right. Your dads aren't there, are they? And the Festers are only blowing up the forecourt. They'll be safe."

"Dads? Disgusting!" said Flakie. "He must be one of them fancy-pants boys. You one of them, too?" He glared at Bo accusingly.

"No. Not me," said Bo. "And not Callum either." She looked warningly at him, hoping he'd understand her meaning and keep his mouth shut.

"Tell us more about Roc," she said.

"I told you. He finds us and he leads us. He's our captain."

"Like Peter Pan?" said Bo.

"What mob does he lead? I never heard of no Pan," said Blister.

"It's a good story. Do you want me to tell it to you?"

"Tell us what?"

"A story," said Bo, settling down on the edge of the dock with her feet dangling over the water. She indicated for the boys to sit next to her. "Stories make the time pass quickly."

Blister and Flakie sat very still, puzzled, as Bo began to speak. Callum shuffled a little way along the dock, as far away from the Festers as he could be and still remain within earshot.

When Bo reached the part where Peter Pan convinced the children they could fly, Flakie interrupted her. "You met this Peter Pan dude yourself? You been to this Never Land?" he asked. "I reckon Roc would like to know about this."

"No," said Bo. "It's not a real place and Peter Pan isn't a real person."

"So it's all a lie. A big fib, eh?"

"No, it's a story. About how things might be."

The Festers nodded solemnly, and Bo went back to telling them about the Lost Boys, their captain who could fly, and their home in Never Land.

20
Roc's Diseases

It was hot and stuffy inside the sub. Although there were windows along the side and front, darkness pressed in around them. Bo and Callum were jammed into a corner where Roc could keep an eye on them.

"Take-off," said Roc, and the sub plunged downward with a sickening surge. He turned to Bo and Callum. "We'll be in the harbor tunnel soon. Then home in no time."

The tiny light at the front of the sub barely lit the way through the tunnel. Callum cupped his hands together and whispered into Bo's ear, "I don't like this plan. We shouldn't be doing this. Festers give me the creeps. And that Roc is bad news."

Bo watched Roc as he leaned over the controls and gave instructions to Blister. He looked like a man. His arm muscles were bigger than any of the others, and his face, though still boyish, had a hard, adult cast to its features. Though his skin was a golden tan, every hair on his body was blond. Even his eyebrows were white-blond. The other Festers were mostly dark and scruffy-looking but there was something sleek and disturbing about Roc.

A pinprick of light appeared in the soupy harbor waters. The sub lurched to one side and passed through a hole in the tunnel. They surfaced near the end of a stone pier that jutted out into a cove from a mass of broken rock. Blister and Flakie opened the hatch at the top of the submarine and the boys scrambled up into the daylight. Bo drew in long, warm breaths of the outside air with relief. It smelled sharp with the tang of the eucalyptus.

The boys pulled a mass of broken branches over the edge of the pier and covered the moored sub so that from a distance it merged with the ragged landscape.

While the other boys climbed a narrow trail into the bush, Roc held Bo back. They stood on the end of the pier, Mr. Pinkwhistle between them. Roc squatted down beside him.

"Where did you get this? I used to have a toy that looked like one of these, but it stopped working and no one knew how to fix it."

"Mr. Pinkwhistle is not a toy," said Bo. "We hunt together." She snapped her fingers and Mr. Pinkwhistle jumped into her arms.

Roc looked up and noticed Callum, glaring at the edge of the trail.

"Hey, Scab," he called. "Come here."

Callum climbed back down onto the dock. "My name is Callum, not Scab."

"If you're going to be a Fester you need a real name."

"I don't want to be a Fester. I don't need to live off garbage. I was chosen. I have two fathers who are happy to raise me. Tomorrow, me and Bo are going to find them," said Callum.

"Maybe you will," said Roc, smiling coldly. "But if you don't, you'll need me. Remember what I named you when you come crawling back and ask for my help."

"And you," he said, taking one of Bo's hands and pulling her close to him so she could feel his warm breath on her face, "you can be Ebola. You'll make a lethal Disease."

A shout from one of the younger boys caught Roc's attention and, with a nod to Bo, he pushed past Callum and sauntered away, following his Festers up the winding trail.

"What a strange boy," said Bo.

"Strange? Psycho's more like it," said Callum.

"I think he's interesting."

"You thought Mollie Green was interesting."

Bo ignored him and set off along the trail, following Roc. Callum grabbed her by the arm.

"How can you be so smart and so dumb at the same time? We shouldn't have come with them. Those Festers, they probably want to barbecue us for their dinner."

"You have to take a chance on people sometimes," said Bo. "I took a chance on you when I found you in the desert."

"Yes, but I am not a Fester. You can't give yourself away to everyone. Festers are factory fodder gone feral."

"No, they're people. Like you and me."

"They're not like me. My fathers chose me."

"People are people. Where we come from isn't as important as who we choose to become."

"Once a freak, always a freak."

"Like me?" said Bo sharply. She strode ahead of him, catching up to the tribe of Festers. She followed the path the boys had made and emerged from the scrub onto a wide, cracked blacktop road. Piles of rubble lay strewn along the broken sidewalks and weeds and vines sprang up through every crack. Unlike the ravaged city on the south side, everything on the north side was covered with a mantle of green. Nature was reclaiming the landscape. They crossed a stream that flowed swiftly over the side of a crumbling stone wall and turned into the driveway of a dilapidated mansion. The glass was broken in most of the windows and the front entrance was a gaping cavern, but the boys tramped inside regardless. Roc was waiting on the threshold for Bo.

"This is our base for the moment. The North Shore is full of empty old places. We move around a lot so the Colony can't track us, but we meet here to plan our attacks."

Inside the mansion, Bo discovered Festers camped in every room. Every corner was filled with crowds of boys. The air reverberated with their voices as they crowed Roc's name, acknowledging his return. He led Bo to the rear of the building and they passed through broken French doors into an overgrown garden.

A boy with a mane of russet hair sat on the edge of an old swimming pool with a net, fishing the lily-covered water. Farther, in a clearing beyond the pool, an area that was once tennis courts, boys were hauling bracken and wood into a huge pile.

"Hey, Festie," called Roc.

The boy who was fishing secured his line and then jogged over to join them.

"This is my baseman," said Roc. "He runs the place when I'm away. Festie, I found a new Disease. I've named him Ebola."

Festie's right arm hung limply by his side but he slapped Bo firmly on the shoulder with his strong left hand. He smiled at her, his expression warm and welcoming. At that moment, Callum came charging across the garden, skidding to a stop beside Bo.

"Thanks for waiting for me," he said.

"This is Callum," said Bo.

Roc looked at her coldly. "No, he's Scab."

"Ebola and Scab?" asked Festie.

"I'm Callum, he's Bo," said Callum, looking at Roc pointedly. "There's no one called Scab or Ebola."

"We used to have a Scab," said Festie, looking confused. "We lost him a few weeks back. I thought you'd come to take his place. Your name needs to show you belong."

"Maybe we don't belong here," said Callum.

Roc frowned and turned on him. "Look, you're lucky I brought you here. You can go back to the city and get gunned down, you can head out into the scrub and get baited or starve for all I care."

Roc walked away and was immediately surrounded by a swarm of small boys demanding his attention.

"You shouldn't wind him up," said Festie. "We'd all be dead without him. He's the boss around here."

"He's not our boss," said Callum.

"You should wish he was," replied Festie.

Callum folded his arms across his chest and looked away. Bo wanted to shake him but she turned to Festie instead. She liked his pale, freckled face, his gentle manner. She felt she could trust him.

"Roc means a lot to you," she said.

"I was the first boy he saved. He fished me out of a dumpster, brought me here. Made me whole again. He's saved hundreds since me."

"What do you mean 'saved'?" asked Bo.

"I was dying." He pushed up his sleeve and displayed his shriveled, twisted right arm. "He called me Festie cause I smelled bad—rotting flesh and all. But he healed me. He used to fish us wounded boys out of dumpsters when we were given up for dead, bring us over to the North Shore, and give us time to heal. Now he don't need to do that anymore. Now we got runaways, dumpster kids, all types. Lots of them are whole. Not like me."

Bo gently touched Festie's scars.

"What were you doing in a dumpster?"

"When drones get injured bad or too sickly to work,

the boss men chuck them in dumpsters. They're not supposed to but it happens all the time. Drones don't count as anything to the Colony."

"You can't be a drone," said Callum. "Drones are made from pigs and sheep. They're not the same as regular people. They're not like us."

"Where did you hear that garbage?" asked Festie.

Bo looked across the pool at the crowd of boys foraging beneath the trees. Were they really made from pigs and sheep?

"You two need to know your place," said Festie. "It don't matter how you was brewed. It's what you do that counts." He turned to Callum. "Ebola, he has to go on missions with Roc 'cause that's what Diseases do. If Roc reckons you're Scab, means you're a Clot, like me. We stay here at the base and help look after the wounded and the little ones. That's what Clots do. We make everything stick together."

"I'm not staying! And what is it with these gross names, Ebola and Scab, Blister and Flakie? They sound disgusting."

"They're meant to. They're meant to make you think. See, we're like sores on the skin of Vulture's Gate. That's why Roc gives us names like that. He says we're a scourge and that once the Diseases become like a plague, we'll get rid of all the men who hurt boys, and make the city for the young ones, the way it should be."

"But everyone grows old one day," said Bo.

"Not us," said Festie. "We're brewed different. Genetically manured."

"He means genetically manufactured," said Callum.

Festie kept his focus on Bo, ignoring Callum. "Roc says most of us GM boys will be lucky to get twenty years. He knows how boys get cooked. He was a Colony kid."

"I don't believe you. I don't believe any of this," said Callum. He ran away from them, beating his way through the grass with a stick. Bo watched him until he stopped in the shade of a giant Moreton Bay fig tree and slumped in the tangle of roots at its base. All of a sudden, she wondered if she'd been right to persuade him to come with the Festers.

Apologizing to Festie, she followed the path Callum had beaten through the long grass. When she knelt beside him, he put his arms around her neck and pulled her close.

"Did you tell Roc?" he whispered in her ear. "Did you tell him you're really a girl?"

"No."

"I think he knows," said Callum. "Why else would he want you to be one of his Diseases?"

Bo frowned. "Because he likes me and I like him."

Callum scowled and pushed her away. "You like him? He's a killer!"

"He's not like an Outstationer," argued Bo. "I think he wants to do good things for these boys and make a proper home for them."

"But we don't need him. If we can find my fathers, we'll have our own proper home."

Bo drew a deep breath. She didn't want to say it but she had to make Callum face the truth. "What if we can't find your fathers? They weren't at the Tower. We don't know where they are. Perhaps, for now, we do need Roc. Perhaps we should be his friend."

"You don't want someone like Roc to be your friend. You don't need him. You have me."

Bo sighed. She put Mr. Pinkwhistle on the ground beside her and drew Callum close. "You are my first friend, Cal. There will never be anyone like you. You will always be my first."

Callum went limp in her arms and buried his face against her neck.

"I'm so tired," he said. "I wish it was night so we could lie down and sleep. I wish we were still in the desert, just the two of us."

They lay entwined for a long time, listening to the peaceful sound of each other's breathing. Suddenly, Bo was aware that someone was watching. She looked up into the branches of the Moreton Bay fig. In every bough of the tree, a small boy sat watching. Scores of small faces stared down at them. Callum followed her gaze and groaned.

"I hate this place," he muttered. He grabbed Bo's hand and dragged her away from the watchers, into the bright, harsh sunlight.

21
Dancing with the Festers

They spent what was left of the afternoon wandering through the garden, exploring the rooms of the dilapidated mansion. Boys were clustered everywhere. Some lay curled up asleep on battered mattresses in the ballroom. Others were at work in the messy kitchen, sorting through piles of fruit and seeds. Everywhere Bo looked, Festers were busily doing chores. All through the day, hordes of them tramped in and out of the mansion with armloads of food that they had caught or foraged in the scrub.

Late in the afternoon, a messenger came to tell Bo that Roc wanted to see her in the old chapel. It was almost dark when Bo and Callum found the ruined building. It was buried under a tangle of blackberries. Inside, Roc and the boys he called his Diseases were having a meeting. When

Roc saw Bo and Callum at the door he gestured them inside.

"Scab, you should be in the ballroom with the other Clots. Report back to Festie."

"He's with me for now," said Bo. "I need him."

Roc ignored her remark but slapped the ground beside him, indicating she should sit. She glanced around the room, at the small assortment of weapons in one corner and the tangle of wires, explosives, and paraphernalia piled in the middle of the chapel. Several of the boys were attempting to unravel some of the wiring but she could tell they weren't adept at their task.

"Is this your munitions store?" she asked.

Roc frowned and kept his gaze down as he spoke.

"We need a better method of detonating the bombs. The way we're doing it isn't good enough," he said. "We lost Scurvy today. He was placing a bomb and it detonated too soon. It took years to get this tribe strong. We don't want to lose any more of the older boys. Especially not any of you Diseases."

Bo squatted down beside Roc and tapped Mr. Pinkwhistle on his spine. The roboraptor ambled forward, pushing his snout into the tangle of wires and pulling a piece of slapper foil from the pile.

Carefully, Bo smoothed the foil between her fingers. "This could be helpful," she said, handing the foil to Roc.

"You know something about explosives?"

"A little bit," she said. She raked through the wires on the floor and then examined the prototype bomb that Roc had devised. She looked at the fuses and the detonators and shook her head. "Most of this is useless. Or dangerous. You should be using a chemical detonator to time the explosions, not all these dinky mechanical ones. If you design it properly, your enemies' sensors won't find it so easily."

Roc and the other boys listened attentively as Bo showed them a better technique for assembling their blasting caps. Every now and then, she glanced at Callum, wishing he'd sit down beside her instead of standing awkwardly near the doorway.

As it grew darker in the chapel, the boys began to drift out into the night garden but Roc and Bo stayed on, locked in conversation. Suddenly Bo realized everyone was gone except Callum.

Roc stood up and dusted off his hands. "We should go. Tonight we have our Last Day celebration. The boys will be waiting to start. We have to move on tomorrow."

"What about all this?" asked Bo, gesturing toward the munitions.

"The Diseases will take care of it. We move regularly so the Colony can't track us. The Worms are in charge of finding new homes."

"Who?"

"Two brothers. We call them Tape and Ring." Bo scrunched up her nose and Roc laughed. "When you meet them, you'll understand. It suits them."

In the fading light, Bo hurriedly lined up the tins and packets of chemicals that were scattered around the chapel, checking the supplies one last time. "You need to add some mercury fulminate to this lot. Can you forage some?"

"You can't scavenge any of this stuff. We have to buy it."

"Who from?" asked Bo.

"I have my sources. But they want gold. You can't barter for weaponry and explosives."

"We have some gold. You can have it. We haven't used it," said Bo, turning to Callum expectantly.

Callum was outraged. He clutched his belt, covering the green leather wallet with both hands. "Forget it! I'm not giving him my gold! He wants to blow up the Colony, Bo. I'm not helping him."

"You don't have to give me anything," said Roc. "I could take it from you if I wanted."

Bo instantly regretted her suggestion. She stood up and crossed the chapel to stand beside Callum. "I'm on Callum's side. If he doesn't want to help you, then neither do I."

Roc put his hands on his hips. "Listen, boy," he said, looking straight at Callum, "I'm not your enemy. I grew up in the Colony, too. I understand you better than you think. You're scared I'm going to hurt your old men. But I'm not interested in destroying South Head right now. There are factions in the city that trade in lost boys and run sweatshops where kids work until they drop. They're my next target, and they're enemies of the Colony. Haven't you heard that saying 'My enemy's enemy is my friend'? For now, we're on the same side."

"Flakie said you're going to bring down the Nekhbet Tower," said Callum.

"Most of the Colony have abandoned it so you shouldn't care. Your old men are probably on South Head. So I'll cut you a deal. I'll leave the Tower alone for now and help you get into the Colony."

"Why would you help me?"

"If you have gold, we can make an exchange. My knowledge for your stash."

"You said you could take it."

"I'm not a bully. I'm a leader. I never force a boy to do anything if I can bargain with him first."

Bo put one arm around Callum. "Do what you think is right," she said. Even though Callum's expression was fiercely angry, she could feel him hesitating. Suddenly she realized how much she wanted him to part with the gold. She bit her tongue to stop herself from arguing Roc's case. Mr. Pinkwhistle started to growl and his spine undulated with anxiety. Bo knew he was sensing the tension in the air: fear, uncertainty, and indecision.

Callum untied the green leather bag from his belt and threw it at Roc's feet.

"Good call," said Roc. "Let's go and join the celebration."

Behind the dilapidated mansion, in the open space that was once the tennis courts, the Festers had built a bonfire. Teams of bigger boys stood raking the coals at the edge of the fire, while the small ones picked among the ashes, flicking smoldering chunks onto container lids.

"Dinner," said Roc, inviting Callum and Bo to join a

group squatting around a wide dish covered with small, smoking brown lumps.

Bo reached down and picked one up. It smelled warm and nutty but it was hard to identify by firelight.

"Try it," said Roc.

Callum picked one up, too, and popped it in his mouth. "Crunchy," he said.

"Mine's chewy. Chewy and nutty," said Bo, reaching for another. "What is it?"

"Roasted cicada," said Roc. "Maybe a few roasted crickets, too—they're the crunchy ones. Cicada's mostly chewy." He scooped up a handful of bugs and crammed them into his mouth.

Callum gagged and spat a mangled cricket back into his hand, but Bo took another cicada and bit it in half. Roc smiled at her, his pale eyes sparkling in the firelight.

When the meal was finished, the Festers threw more timber on the bonfire, building it high. Some boys went to sit in the trees, some in the long grass, or they clustered in small groups on the edge of the tennis court. Suddenly, as one, they all began to hum. The sound rose up into the night air like the whirr of small wings.

Festie picked up a stick and began to slowly tap out a rhythm on a broken tin. Then Roc walked to the front of the crowd with four of the other boys and started to clap a different rhythm that worked in and around the beat Festie was drumming.

Bo tipped her head to one side and listened closely. The rhythms made her heart change its pace. When the beat was established, six of the bigger boys started to make a deeper humming noise that rolled under all the other sounds. Bo's skin felt warm, as if the sound were making it tingle. Tier after tier of boys joined in with their own cries, while the steady beat of Festie's makeshift drum wove in and out of the voices and around the clapping.

Boys began to tap their feet and move slowly to the music. Because that was what it must be, thought Bo, even though she'd never heard anything like it before. Music. Each note unlocked something deep inside. Her throat throbbed. She shut her eyes and let the sounds enfold her.

Callum began to sing, too, his voice warm and honey-sweet. His song wove its way around every part of Bo. Tears seeped out of her eyes, streamed down her dirty face, and dripped from her chin.

"What's happening? What's wrong with me?" she asked. She was trembling. Her breath came in short gasps that made her chest ache. "Is this the plague? Is this what it does to you?"

Callum stopped singing and cupped one hand under Bo's chin, catching the cascade of tears. He looked into her eyes and smiled.

"It's all right, Bo. You're only crying."

"Girls don't cry," she said, wiping her hand across her eyes. "Only boys cry!"

"Everybody cries sometime. Just let it happen."

As the song grew stronger, some of the boys began to stamp their feet and move in time to the music. Without understanding the impulse, Bo found her feet moving, too. It was as if the music and the tears were making things happen to her body, things she had no control over. Almost unconsciously, she found herself dancing alongside the Festers. Her tears stopped and she started to laugh, twirling through the long grass with Callum by her side. She looked up at the night sky, at the swirl of stars above. They were paler than those that hung above Tjukurpa Piti but they were the same familiar constellations. It was like a sign: a promise that here, among these wild boys, she could make a home.

Callum spun past her and for a moment she was stricken. She watched him as he jumped in time to the music, clapping his hands and stamping his feet. How could she explain to him that the idea of being locked inside the Colony with his fathers made her want to run away? How could she tell him that the thought of living without the open sky above her, without this crazy tribe of children to dance with, made her feel as if all the light inside her was extinguished? How was she going to convince him to stay?

22
Lifeblood

Bo woke early to the sound of birds. The dawn chorus sent a shiver coursing through her body. She had been dreaming of birds, of the fluttering of their wings near her face, of their sharp beaks and their beady eyes. She sat up and clutched her string bag of weapons. Beside her, Callum snuffled sleepily and turned away, back into his dreams. Quietly, she stepped over the sleeping bodies of Festers. Some boys were already up and hunting, crawling through the long grass in search of bugs and grubs for breakfast.

The new mansion was smaller than the last, with rooms opening onto a central courtyard. Far below lay a serpentine stretch of blue harbor. Bo was mystified at how the water had purchase in every corner of Vulture's Gate. It felt as though the harbor was edging up against the city, waiting to pull it back into the sea. She pushed her way through the tangled undergrowth to a lookout point. Dewdrops glistened on the tips of wild grasses. On the edge of the cliff, Bo saw Blister in the boughs of an overgrown apricot tree reaching for a piece of high fruit. Suddenly he fell, his back arching. There was a sickening thud as he hit the ground.

"Blister?" she called, running.

His body was twitching and a froth of orange foam spilled from his mouth. She knelt down and tried to hold him but his limbs thrashed wildly and his eyes rolled back in his head. Suddenly, he lay still and limp. She slipped her arms beneath him and carried him to the house, calling for Festie. But it was Roc who met her as she came staggering up the pathway.

"Blister," he said, taking the small boy from her. "Not Blister." His face twisted in grief.

"He was in the tree and then he fell and then he started twitching and . . ."

Roc cradled Blister's head against his chest and sniffed his breath.

"Baited," he said. "We'll have to move again. They know we're here." His eyes were hard. He carried Blister back to the apricot tree and laid him gently beside its trunk.

"We must bury him," said Bo.

"No," said Roc. "We leave him here so other boys know this tree isn't safe."

"Can't we leave a warning sign instead? You can't simply let the birds and animals eat Blister!"

"Most of the boys can't read. And the poison is made for boys, not beasts."

Bo looked at Roc in disbelief. "I wasn't worried about the animals. This is Blister. Your friend. You can't leave him like this."

Roc lifted one arm up to his face and covered his eyes.

"We need to get the boys moving," he said in a muffled voice. "I've made a mistake."

Bo followed him back to the house. She found Callum standing on the stone steps of the patio, while a tiny boy tugged at his hand.

Bo bent down and swept the restless toddler into her arms. She pushed her face against his warm, soft neck.

"Bo," said Callum insistently, "what's going on?"

"Blister is dead," she replied. "The Festers are moving again."

"We don't have to go with them," said Callum. "We can go and find my dads. That's why we came to Vulture's Gate, remember?"

"Didn't you hear me?" she said. "Blister is *dead*."

Callum blushed. "I'm sorry. I'm sorry he's gone. But we're not Festers, Bo."

"Maybe I am," she answered.

Callum was about to respond when Roc came over and spoke directly to Bo. "Leave that kid," he said. "He's too little. We don't take the smallest ones."

"But he can't take care of himself."

"We've got too many littlies already. Festie should never have fished that one out of the dumpster. He's too small."

"Like Festie when you found him," said Bo, shifting the toddler onto her hip. But Roc was already striding away, shouting instructions at the boys milling in the courtyard.

Festie pushed his way over to join Bo and Callum. He tickled the baby boy, who stretched out his arms for Festie to hold him.

"Hello, little Bug," said Festie. "I called him Bug 'cause he was right down in the bottom of the bin, scrabbling around like a crazy thing. He'll be the lifeblood of the Festers one day. Don't know why he was thrown away. He's perfect. Maybe he had dads who changed their minds so they put him out with the garbage."

"Men from the Colony wouldn't do that," said Callum.

"Sure they would," said Festie. "You one of those Festers with fancy-schmancy ideas about how Colony dads operate?"

"No, but I have two dads that love me," said Callum.

Festie laughed and raised his eyebrows skeptically.

"Then what are you doing here?"

"I'm leaving. We're going to find my fathers today."

"Sounds like that 'Once upon a time' story Bo was telling last night," said Festie. "Once upon a time a boy tried to go back to his dads that abandoned him and when they saw him again, they put him back in the garbage. . . . Festers make better fathers than Colony men. Festers stick up for the underdogs."

"So why does Roc say we have to leave this Bug of yours behind?" asked Callum.

157

Festie blanched. "Roc never said that."

"Ask him," said Callum.

Bo stepped between the two boys and pushed them apart.

"You are both utterly annoying," said Bo. "Give me back the Bug. I'll carry him."

She didn't wait for either of the boys to join her but Callum fell in step as she headed out of the mansion, following the snaking line of boys onto the wide road. Roc was at the front but when he looked over and saw Bo he strode back down the line, his expression like thunder.

"I told you to leave that one behind," he said.

"I don't mind carrying him," said Bo. "Callum and Festie will share him with me."

"That's not the point!" said Roc. "It's time to cull the little ones."

"Roc," said Bo, putting a hand on his arm. "It's all right. We can do this."

Roc shook her hand away. "Don't tell me what's going to happen. I say what's going to happen, not you."

"I know you're upset about Blister . . ."

"Boys die all the time. You'll die, too. And faster if you keep arguing with me."

Bo blushed angrily and Mr. Pinkwhistle, sensing her distress, scurried in front of her, bobbing from one leg to the other, his eyes flashing red as he monitored Roc's position and prepared to attack.

Roc looked down in irritation. Then he drew back his leg and kicked the roboraptor hard in the chest, sending him flying. Mr. Pinkwhistle landed on the road and scudded across the bitumen, coming to a stop near a spiky hedge. Even though he landed hard on his spine, he pivoted around to charge again. Bo's whistle stopped him in his tracks. He stood, bewildered, nodding his head, waiting for the signal to attack.

"I'm sorry he attacked. I won't let him hurt you," said Bo.

Roc snorted in derision. "As if that piece of crap could do me any damage. It's as big a disappointment as you are," he said. "I thought you were going to be useful."

Bo narrowed her eyes. "And I thought you cared about things that mattered, that you were doing something important."

Roc clenched his fists and leaped on her, knocking her to the ground. Bug went tumbling into the air and Bo cried out, "Bug! Someone catch him."

Callum jumped forward and caught the toddler before he hit the ground. Bug began to wail as Callum shoved him into Festie's arms and then threw himself on Roc's back. The Festers were instantly upon him as he struggled to get Roc in a headlock. They dragged Callum clear while Bo fought like a wildcat. But Roc was almost man-sized, and he used his fists without remorse. In minutes, he had her pinned firmly to the ground. She licked away a trail of blood from the side of her mouth and snarled at him.

"Do you feel better now? Now that you've shown you can bully me any time you like? What happened to 'I never *force* a boy to do anything?'"

Roc trembled with rage. "Why can't you shut up!"

He scanned the crowd. A group of Festers had caught

Mr. Pinkwhistle. One boy had his tail, two held his body, and a fourth threw a piece of cloth over his head and held him fast. Beside them, three other boys had Callum pinned to the ground.

"Look, we've got your mate, we've got your machine, and we've got you. So from now on, you do as I say," said Roc.

Bo looked straight into Roc's angry face and spat. It landed on his cheekbone and slithered down to his chin. Even though her mouth was full of blood, she smiled.

Then they heard the copters. Black against the pale blue morning sky, they swooped low over the roadway. With a collective cry of terror, the Festers dispersed into the undergrowth. Some scrambled up trees, others disappeared into the nearest tumble-down house. The boys holding down Callum released him and scurried into the bush.

Roc leaped up and grabbed Bo's hands, dragging her to her feet. "Run!" was all he said. But even as he spoke, the nets were falling. Heavy wire mesh dropped from the copters, blanketing the streetscape and covering any boy unlucky enough to still be out in the open.

The copters landed on the broken road, and drones opened fire with long-range Tasers. Bo ducked. She could hear a surging, pumping noise inside her head and knew it was the sound of her own fear. She whistled for Mr. Pinkwhistle but he had vanished.

On the street, chaos reigned. Squadrones were firing into the bush, Tasering runaways, untangling boys from nets, and rounding up the ones that were still writhing from the pain of being Tasered. Roc stood stock-still, his face a mask, as the captured Festers gathered around him. Bo scanned the crowd of defeated boys, searching the faces of the captured, hoping Callum had escaped.

As the Squadrones closed in on the boys, she saw a flicker of movement inside a tangle of fallen branches in a nearby garden. Suddenly, Callum leaped over a fence and ran toward her, his hands in the air to signal his surrender.

"Callum," she said, as he fell into line beside her, "what have you done?"

"I couldn't let them take you. I couldn't let them take you without me."

23
Sheep from the Goats

Bo, Callum, and Roc said nothing to each other as they sat side by side on the roadside, waiting. Six Squadrones were left with them while the other copters took off into the blue morning sky. Bo glanced along the row of captured boys. She spotted Flakie at the end but Festie and Bug were nowhere in sight. Close to thirty of the Festers were missing, and she could only hope they had made it to safer ground.

The Squadrones hadn't bothered pursuing anyone into the bush, satisfied with their haul of fifty boys. They circled their prisoners like crows but came no nearer than to nudge a boy with a boot or threaten them with a Taser if they tried to speak to each other.

"Stay awake," whispered Roc. "If you fall asleep, they

might think you're sickly and shoot you. They only want the strong ones."

Bo sat up straight and eyed the Squadrones angrily, but inside she was churning with guilt. She knew that if she and Roc hadn't been fighting they might have been more alert to the threat. They might have been able to bolt into the surrounding gardens and disappear into a ravine before the nets fell. And Callum—if it hadn't been for her wanting to stay with the Festers, they might be with Callum's fathers by now, and yet, despite everything he'd still come back for her.

When the truck finally arrived, it looked more like a four-wheel-drive bus than an armored vehicle. The Festers were herded on board and driven along bumpy, cracked roads to the edge of the North Shore. The sun beat down on the roof and inside everyone began to sweat. When Bo reached up to open a window, a Squadrone hit the back of her hand, grazing her knuckles with the butt of his gun.

The boys were off-loaded behind the ruins of an old amusement park. The wind whipped off the harbor and Bo licked her lips, tasting salt. So much water. It made her uneasy, left her wondering how the land could compete with the sea, with the relentless pounding of surf against rocks, the constant erosion of the ground they walked upon. It was as if everything in Vulture's Gate was under attack.

They went into a large white building with a sign above the doorway that read ROT, and then beneath, in smaller letters REORIENTATION TERMINAL. A man in a white coat came out and inspected the Festers, checking to see if any of them were wounded and scanning them for microchips. "Time to sort the sheep from the goats," he said, smiling grimly.

Bo could tell he wasn't a drone. His eyes were bright and sharp and he shouted instructions to the Squadrones, ordering them to separate the boys into groups.

Bo watched Callum fingering the crescent-shaped scars on his ears. He blended so perfectly with the Festers, it would be hard to believe he wasn't one of them. She wondered if he would try and explain to the man in the white coat that he was from the Colony but he stepped closer to Bo and kept his head down. Then it dawned on her: If he told them his story, they would be separated. She slipped her hand into his and their fingers entwined.

Flakie and two other boys were dragged away as the microchip scanner registered their histories. The small boys were sorted from the older ones and led down a long, brightly lit corridor. Roc kept his head up, his face proud, but he would not look at any of the boys.

"What will they do to them?" asked Bo.

"Flakie and the other chipped boys are runaways. They'll go back to the men who own them. The little ones I don't want to think about," said Roc. He looked across at her with hollow eyes. All Bo's rage against him drained away. She touched his hand. He was nothing like the angry golden boy she'd fought on the road.

They were organized into single file and marched down another hallway into a long bathroom where showerheads jutted out above them from every wall. A large black bin was wheeled into the center of the room. Squadrones positioned themselves in every corner, breaking up clusters of boys, forcing Bo and Callum to step apart.

"Strip," said one of the Squadrones. "Throw all your clothes in the bin and stand under one of the showers. Now!"

"They're going to kill us," said Roc, grimly stripping off his shirt.

"Why didn't they simply shoot us when they caught us?" whispered Bo.

Roc shrugged. "Maybe they need us for body parts."

Bo grimaced and began to untie the stays of her ragged shirt. Then she stopped. She watched the boys begin to strip, her mind churning. How could she expose herself in front of them all? Finally everyone was naked except for her. Slowly, she took off her shirt and folded her arms across her chest to cover her breasts, but she still wore a pair of baggy khaki pants that Mollie Green had given her. Callum immediately stepped in front of her, shielding her from view.

"Bo can't take his gear off," he announced. "'Cause his skin is really sensitive."

A Squadrone pushed through the crowd of boys, shoved Callum out of the way, and pulled out a long knife. In one swift movement he cut through Bo's trousers so the fabric fell away and lay in pieces around her ankles. Bo shut her eyes. One boy cried out, "What's wrong with him?" Then she felt a pair of strong hands grip her shoulders and shake her hard. She opened her eyes to see Roc glaring at her.

"You lied to me," he said, his voice full of hurt. "Why didn't you say?"

Callum pushed between them.

"She's a girl. That's all. See, they're not all gone. We have to help her. We have to keep her safe," he said pleadingly to the other boys.

He was shouldered aside. A tall and powerfully built drone swept Bo into his arms and carried her through the startled press of naked boys. At the doorway, she was wrapped in a blanket and slung over the shoulder of another Squadrone. As the sound of the boys receded, the last voice she heard was Callum's, calling her name, sharp and insistent. "Bo! Bo! Bo!"

24
Mater Misericordiae

Bo could hardly breathe. A prickly blanket smothered her face, and she wriggled and clawed at the fabric until she made a tiny opening through which she could see. She was inside one of the small copters that Callum had called a Pally-val, and they were flying high over the water. Beneath them was an island, in the middle of the harbor, between the ruined city and the overgrown North Shore. Sheer stone walls rose straight up from the water making the island impregnable by sea. The copter landed in a walled garden in the center of the island.

As soon as the Pally-val touched down, Bo was hauled over someone's shoulder, rolled out of the blanket, and deposited naked on her back on a stretch of smooth green lawn. She drew her knees up to her chest and made herself small. Three strangers in long robes stared down at her.

Their faces were soft and narrow, framed by tight wimples. Their lips were painted soft pink and their eyebrows were shaped in perfect crescents. They looked like characters from a storybook. They looked like women.

One of the women reached down and tried to drag Bo to her feet but Bo pulled away. She wanted to bare her teeth, to snarl at them like Mr. Pinkwhistle. The thought of Mr. Pinkwhistle sent a wave of grief coursing through her.

The oldest woman spoke. She was as weathered as Mollie Green, her face lined, her long eyelashes silvery gray.

"Come inside, child. You can't sit here naked in the sunlight forever."

Grudgingly, Bo got to her feet. The woman tried to take her hand but Bo tucked them under her armpits and let the blanket trail along the ground behind her.

They crossed the lawn and climbed the steps of a shiny, shell pink and silver building. In the foyer, a copper sign read MATER MISERICORDIAE.

Once the sliding glass doors of the building had shut behind them, the women took off their black cloaks. Beneath them they wore pale blue silk dresses that accentuated their hips and breasts. Their long, shining hair cascaded over their shoulders, reminding Bo of the queens and princesses she had seen in fairy-tale illustrations. They led Bo down bright corridors in silence, hemming her in on all sides. Bo tried to mask her curiosity but she couldn't help glancing around at the strangeness of her surroundings. Nothing was broken in this building. Everything was clean and smooth and the air was heavy with cloying perfumes.

The older woman opened a door to a large, airy room and then gestured for Bo to enter. She pointed to a plush white sofa beneath a barred window.

"You may be seated," she said.

Bo remained standing.

"You have nothing to fear. You are in safe hands now. I am Alethea, and this is Verity and Meera," she said, gesturing to each of the two other women. "Do you have a name, child?"

Bo stayed stubbornly mute. She registered a flicker of annoyance in the old woman's expression. "Later, then," said Alethea. She nodded to the other two women and left the room.

"We will help you wash," said Meera.

"No!" said Bo. "I can clean myself!"

The two women looked at each other and smiled, which Bo found inexplicably annoying. They bowed in assent and led her into the bathroom, where they demonstrated how to use the faucets and shower. Then they left her alone.

As soon as the door closed behind them, Bo felt her body relax. At last she could think. She came out of the bathroom and sat on the end of the bed. It was impossibly soft. Everything about the room was soothing. The walls were painted pale green and the dusky beige carpet felt lush beneath her bare feet. Bo went back into the bathroom and touched the smooth white tiles. Every surface was so bright, so clean and shiny, that it almost hurt her eyes.

Most alarming of all was a huge mirror that covered an entire wall of the bathroom. Now that she was alone she stood in front of it and stared at her reflection. Her hair was matted at the back and tangled into long rattails at the front. She felt startled by her own green eyes staring back at her. There had been a small mirror at Tjukurpa Piti but she had never seen her whole body. It didn't look the way she had expected. The budding breasts and the tiny patch of silky dark hair at her crotch seemed as if they should belong to someone else. She bared her teeth and was disappointed to see they were discolored and one tooth on the left was sharp and jagged, probably chipped in the crash of the Daisy-May.

She turned on the shower and watched the water spilling onto the tiled floor of the cubicle. It flowed without stopping, like a waterfall, and the water was clear and sparkling, not like the murky brown water of Tjukurpa Piti. She held her hand under it until she was sure there was nothing in it that would hurt her, then she stepped into the silvery flow. The water around the drain swirled brown and red as months of caked grime was washed from her body. Her skin became lighter, like golden honey. She stood beneath the flow until all the dirt had washed away, until even the cracks between her toes were clean.

When she returned to the bedroom wrapped in thick, fluffy towels, she discovered a tray of food on a small table beneath the window. Bo flopped down on the white sofa and stared at the food. Maybe it was poisoned. Maybe now was the time she should try to escape. Although the window was barred, the view was across a garden full of lush plants and bright flowers. Through the foliage, she could see the high, sheer walls that enclosed the island. There would be no easy escape from Mater Misericordiae.

Steam rose from a bowl of soup and beneath a silver cover was a platter of meats and vegetables. Bo sniffed at the food. Her stomach grumbled. There was a small bowl of nuts and a larger one of fruit and a small pink—what? A cupcake? Bo had never eaten a cupcake before, or even seen one, but she had read about them and the cake looked as foolish and wonderful as anything she had imagined. She picked at the icing, which burnt her mouth the same way that Callum's donuts had, and then she picked up a spoon to try the soup. For a moment she hesitated; what if they wanted to kill her? But why would they do it so graciously? The smell of the hot soup was making her stomach ache with hunger. She took a small spoonful and let it rest in her mouth for a minute, savoring the rich, salty flavor.

It took her a long time to finish the food. Part of her wanted to wolf it down, but she knew better than to shock her body with a huge meal. She finished the soup slowly and then tasted a small portion of everything on the other plates. A cozy sleepiness began creeping through her limbs. She lay back on the bed and stared at the ceiling. It was covered in tiny pale pink stars that were oddly hazy. As she gazed at the swirling patterns, all her worries drifted away.

The sheet beneath her felt silky smooth and the covering feather-light yet deliciously warm. She thought back over the events of the afternoon, trying to make sense of what had happened. Her eyes prickled. She pictured Callum and the Festers standing naked in that cold, drab room. When the Squadrone had thrown her so roughly over his shoulder, she thought he was taking her away to be killed. But here she was, lying between silken sheets, being treated like a princess. Through the cloud of her sleepiness, all the stories she'd read of princesses came to her. Princesses who were tricked and deceived, made mute, poisoned, and imprisoned. Princesses who were held hostage by beasts, witches, or ogres. Princesses whose fathers abandoned them and whose stepmothers betrayed them. As sleep came to her, she dreamed of flocks of birds, of brothers turned into swans, and ravens that circled their princess sister, crying out to her for help.

25
The Harmony Enhancement

Callum felt his chest cave in when the doors swung shut behind Bo and the Squadrone, as if he had been gutted alive. He buried his face in his hands and fought back tears.

Roc tapped him on the shoulder.

"You don't have to worry about her," he said bitterly. "She'll be fine. It's us that will suffer."

"What do you mean?"

"They'll take her off to the Island and feed her up like a prize pig, but we're not worth anything to them so they'll kill us. There'll be some sort of poison coming out of those showers any minute."

As if his words were a signal, the showers surged into life. The boys let out one loud collective scream as silvery blue liquid sprayed across their naked bodies. It washed over them until the floor was flooded and they were all standing ankle-deep in the swirling blue.

The liquid smelled tangy and sweet and Callum thought at least dying would smell nice. But no one was looking even faintly ill. They were definitely changing. Some who looked as though they hadn't washed in years, emerged ghostly pale as the dust and dirt was sloughed from their bodies. The room grew steamy, and one of the younger boys started to giggle. Roc looked at him sharply, then at Tape and Ring, who had wide, stupid grins on their faces.

"Cover your nose and mouth!" called Roc, clasping his own hand over his face. "It's the Harmony Enhancement."

"I thought you said they were going to kill us," said Callum, suppressing a giggle.

"I'd rather be dead than harmonized," said Roc, his voice muffled by his hands.

Callum couldn't think what that meant but he covered his face in the same way as Roc and tried not to breathe too deeply.

The water was nearly to their knees by the time the showers were turned off. There was a swirling, sucking sound as a plug opened and the murky water drained away. Callum followed Roc as he pushed his way to the exit. As soon as the drones opened the doors, he took a deep breath of the cool, sour air that flowed into the room.

Callum felt some of the warmth seep out of him as the boys were herded from the showers and into another room where a row of men with clippers stood ready to shear their hair. The Festers, now uncharacteristically cooperative, sat side by side on a long bench as their tangled manes and dreadlocks were shorn off. Callum felt a breeze against his scalp as clumps of his hair fell from his shoulders under the buzz of the shears. When every boy was hairless, they were marshalled into another room where they were given a pair of loose drawstring trousers and a wraparound jacket made of dark brown fabric.

"What did you mean when you said about us being 'harmonized?'" Callum asked Roc.

"That shower was only the beginning," said Roc. "There were chemicals in the water, not just soap. Happy gases that make you think everything is okay."

"Sounds good to me," said Callum, still feeling a remnant of the warm glow that the showers had induced. "It felt good, too."

"No, idiot, it's a living death. You turn into a zombie. You do what they say, and worse, you're happy doing what they say. Next they'll give you pills and jabs to make you mindless, to make you less a man and more a slave. It's called the 'Harmony Enhancement.' It's how they keep everything working in the Colony, how they make men and boys work for nothing. They're filled up with drugs until they forget who they were, until they can't hold other thoughts, other memories. You feel happy all the time. You may as well feel nothing."

Callum sensed the urgency of his earlier despair trying to push through the warm feeling inside him. Suddenly, he understood. He would forget Bo. He would even forget his fathers. The Harmony Enhancement would make him think everything was fine, that everything was as it was meant to be.

"My dads told me something about 'happy men,'" said Callum, fumbling for the memory. "About how they were important for something. But I thought it was a story. Like girls, something they dreamed up," and he laughed, but it was a sharp, angry laugh that made him feel more like his old self.

"My father told me everything," said Roc. "But he told me the truth. It's why I started the Festers. So we could be angry instead of sloppy. Sloppy with happiness."

"You really did have a dad?" asked Callum.

Roc scowled. "You think you're unique? I had two fathers, just like you, and a sister."

"Now I know you're lying. Nobody has a sister."

"You had Bo, didn't you?" said Roc.

"Yeah but she's a freak," said Callum. "The last girl on earth."

"Maybe not."

"Other girls? How can there be other girls?"

"Both my fathers were doctors. They helped make boys—chosen boys like you and me—and fodder as well, boys who would become drones, the Colony worker ants. My dads probably made some of the Festers. Maybe they made you. They brewed and hatched thousands of boys, but girls were what they dreamed of. They couldn't believe their luck when they hatched my sister. When the Colony took her away from us, one of my dads went crazy.

"He started talking too loudly about how women

should be treated equally, how the Colony was corrupt. We tried to make him be quiet but they killed him anyway. Then they killed my other father."

"Who killed them?"

"Colony drones. They were only following orders. The Colony would have made me into a drone, too, but I ran away."

"What happened to your sister?"

"I don't know. I don't even know if I care. If it hadn't been for her, my fathers would still be alive."

Callum took a deep breath and tried to make sense of everything Roc had revealed. He knew Roc was watching for his response but he didn't know what to say.

Finally, he mumbled, "I'm sorry."

"I don't want your sympathy."

"I'm not just sorry for you. I'm sorry for me, too. I always believed that the Colony men were the good guys. Now I don't know what to believe. I don't even know who I am, who you are—what it all means."

Roc sneered. "I know who I am. And I don't care who you are or what you think. I don't care what anyone thinks. But I care about the Festers. The Festers are all equal. We don't need to bring girls back to make things work for us. Boys can grow in glass. They can survive anything. It was the old men that ruined everything, thinking that boys weren't important, treating us like garbage. But no matter how much they try to squash us down, the Festers keep coming back like a disease they can't cure."

A line of docile, shorn boys ambled past them into the

dressing room. "I think they just inoculated against your disease," said Callum.

Roc gripped Callum's arm, pulling him closer. "We have to get them out of here. We have to break out." His blue eyes glittered angrily. "If I can get out with a few boys, I can rally the Festers."

"What do you want me to do?"

"Listen closely," he whispered "They'll try to sedate us in stages. They don't like doing it in one hit, in case they damage our brains. First was the gas, next they'll give us pills. Tomorrow they'll inject us with a cocktail of drugs, send in a whole crew to do the harmonizing. But tonight we still have a chance. When they come with the pills, take them but don't swallow. Hide them under your tongue, or in the side of your mouth. Then, when they ask you to stick your tongue out to prove you've swallowed, do it quickly, but don't let them see the pills. You've got to help me with this. Tell the other boys. As many as you can without making it obvious."

Callum and Roc wove their way through the crowd, trying to look casual as they chatted to the younger boys, leaning on their shoulders and talking cheerfully, as if they were sharing a harmonized joke. Callum figured out the ratio of Squadrones to boys. He didn't like their chances of success. The drones stood in pairs at every exit. Even though their faces were impassive, they kept their Tasers raised, as if waiting for an excuse to fire on the Festers.

Two Squadrones distributed the pills and water. Some boys, who hadn't understood how to keep the pills under their tongue, choked and gulped them down. Others had their mouths squeezed open by the drones and then were roughly slapped to force them to swallow. Callum felt a cold sweat break out all over his body as he threw back the pills and quickly maneuvered them under his tongue.

When the drone passed Callum, they demanded he open his mouth. Somehow, he managed to keep the pills under his tongue as he stuck it out. When he sat on the floor beside Roc, they both pretended to cough, meanwhile flicking the pills into their fists.

"Roc, do you think that if we get out of here I'll be able to find Bo?"

"Bo," said Roc, shaking his head. "I can't believe you."

"What's so funny?"

"You don't want to mess with girls. They're dynamite."

"Bo wasn't toxic. I didn't catch anything from her."

"She was absolutely toxic. You should have traded her for whatever you could get. You had a girl! Every fool wants one."

"You mean sell her?"

"Definitely. Girls are not worth the trouble. They mess with your brain. They ruin everything."

Callum stared up at the ceiling.

"Forget her, Scab. They've probably taken her straight to the Island, to Mater. It's because of Mater Misericordiae that they filled the harbor with mines, to stop anyone getting out there. But one day I'll get there. One day I'll blow the place sky high."

"What about your sister? What if she is on the island?"

"What sort of life could she have out there? I'd be doing her a favor."

Callum felt sick. He didn't want to ask any more questions. He wasn't sure he wanted to hear the answers. All he wanted was to find Bo before it was too late. Once they were together again, they would find his fathers and have them tell the truth. The truth about girls and boys, the truth about the plague, and the truth about the Colony. Slowly, he crushed the pills in his hands until they made a fine, thin dust.

26
Girlfriend

Bo didn't want to wake up. She rolled away from the light that poured in through the barred windows and tried to make her way back into her dream. On the other side, in the darkness of her sleep, she could sense Callum. He had his arms around her waist and they were riding on the Daisy-May across a wide desert with Mr. Pinkwhistle crouched between her knees. All that mattered was the journey.

But something was trying to drag her out of the dream. Slowly, painfully, she came to consciousness. She ached all over and a dull throb in her hips made her groan as she tried to roll over.

"Sleepyhead, wake up," said a voice.

Despite the pain, Bo sat up abruptly, pulling at the blanket to cover herself. "Who are you?"

The girl sitting on the end of her bed was like a fairy

out of a picture book. Her long burnished hair reached to her waist, her teeth were as white as salt, and her lips were shiny pink. She wore a pair of loose turquoise pants and a matching top that reached to her knees. She was smaller than Bo and her face was as soft as a baby's but there was nothing babylike about her expression. She leaned forward conspiratorially.

"I'm Li-Li. I'm going to be your best, best, bestie," she said.

"My beastie?"

"No, silly. Your best, best friend."

Bo remembered when Callum had told her they were best friends, putting his face close to hers and giving her a butterfly kiss. She suddenly imagined what it would feel like if she leaned closer to Li-Li, close enough for the other girl's long, thick black eyelashes to brush against her cheek. She shivered.

"I already have a best friend," she said. "He's called Callum."

Li-Li raised her perfectly shaped eyebrows and laughed. "A boyfriend? Boyfriends can't be best friends."

She slipped off the end of the bed and wandered over to the window. "This is such a pretty room, isn't it? I wish they'd given me this room."

Bo simply grunted in assent and watched the fairy-tale girl through narrowed eyes. Now that she'd recovered from her surprise, the pain was coming back to her. She put one hand to her head and groaned softly. "I hurt. I hurt everywhere."

Li-Li looked at Bo sharply. "You're lucky. Foundlings

are always lucky. I'm a foundling, too. I sailed into the harbor three years ago and they rescued me as my boat was sinking. They say we might be the best variety of girl. We take longer to ripen."

Despite the pain, Bo laughed. "We're not fruit."

"I wasn't making a joke," said Li-Li. She crossed the room and stood over Bo, hands on hips. "I'm here to help you. To help you understand how we live and what's going to happen next. It's all been decided while you were sleeping."

"I haven't decided anything," said Bo, easing herself upright.

This time Li-Li laughed, a high tinkling that Bo thought was the most annoying sound she'd ever heard. "Nothing you decide matters," said Li-Li. "Nothing you decide is important. From now on, everything is decided for you."

The words were barely out of Li-Li's mouth when the door burst open and Alethea entered with Meera and Verity.

"That's enough, Li-Li. We don't want you two to have a spat before you've had a chance to get to know each other."

She smiled as she spoke but she was transparently angry.

"Pooh," said Li-Li, laughing again, and this time her laugh was lighter. She looked over at Bo. "I was only teasing, wasn't I, girlfriend?"

"The child doesn't need to be teased," said Alethea. "She needs our help and support to recover."

Bo fought down her anger. Something had happened to her while she lay sleeping. Something had been done to her, and her body felt fragile.

Meera tried to take Bo's hand but Bo snatched it away. "We're so glad you're feeling better, darling," she said. "I'm sure we're all going to be such good friends."

Bo ignored her, instead directing a question at Alethea.

"Where are the boys, the boys that I was captured with?" she asked.

"They are in safe hands," said Alethea. "But surely, you could not have been with those boys very long. Whoever raised you has kept you intact. He must have been a very fine gentleman to protect you. A Colony man, perhaps?"

Bo understood she was fishing for information but her 'twition told her to give away nothing. "I took care of myself," she said.

"But now we can take care of you," said Meera, putting her hands on Bo's shoulders and staring into her eyes. "Now you can have a real mother. When we cross over to the Colony, I'll be the mother you've always needed. We'll have so much to share with each other."

She tried to kiss Bo on the cheek but Bo recoiled. "I don't want a mother," she said. "Or a new best friend. I want you to let me go and be with the boys."

Everyone laughed, including Li-Li. "When you're feeling recovered and you've had time to get to know us better, you'll feel differently. Once you understand what it means to be a woman, you will be glad to be with your sisters," said Alethea. "For now, Li-Li will help you understand how we do things."

With that, the three women left the room. Meera looked over her shoulder and blew Bo a kiss before pulling the door shut. Bo felt a chill that made her shiver again. She looked down at her naked body, saw bruises on her arms and thighs, and winced at the dull, throbbing ache in her lower back. She wanted to cry but didn't want to give Li-Li the satisfaction or risk Meera coming back to comfort her.

Li-Li sat on the bed, smiling like a Cheshire cat. "Don't mind Meera. She wants to be everyone's mother. Once we've gone back to South Head, you'll feel better. They won't touch you again for a while. I heard Alethea say you were a virgin and didn't need any fixing. Clever you."

"A virgin?"

"You must know what that means!" said Li-Li. "You haven't been with a boy or a man."

"Yes I have," said Bo.

"Not in a way that matters," said Li-Li smugly.

Bo thought of Callum. How could anyone think what they shared didn't matter?

"It's good neither of us is ripe yet. They thought I was but it was a false alarm," said Li-Li, looking at her fingernails.

"What do you mean 'ripe'?" asked Bo, looking down at her washed and scrubbed body. Maybe she should have left the dirt on as a protective layer, to separate herself from these clean, perfectly groomed people.

"Oh nothing," said Li-Li as she looked to the door and frowned. She gestured for Bo to draw closer, then wrapped her arms around Bo's neck and nuzzled close to her ear. "They hear everything we say. When we get away from here I can tell you anything you want to know but you have to be my best friend, okay?"

Bo pulled away and stared at her. She was beautiful, she was strange, and for all her fluffy softness there was a sharpness about Li-Li, like a knife, like a magnet.

"Okay, girlfriend," said Bo.

27
Breakout

"They need to pee," said Roc, pushing Callum and six of the smaller Festers toward a Squadrone. "They all need to pee before they lie down or they'll piss themselves during the night." Roc grinned at the drone as if he was feeling cheerfully "enhanced" and the drone grunted in acknowledgment.

Callum watched Roc carefully as the boys were herded into the urinals, waiting for his cue. Now that the Festers were sedated, only two drones were sent to manage them. He noted a row of louvered windows, like narrow vents, above the urinals.

It happened quickly. One moment Callum was waiting for a signal from Roc, the next Roc had disarmed the first drone, smashing his head against the edge of the urinal. Then he turned the Taser on the other drone, slamming his face against the floor and knocking him senseless before his cries could raise the alarm.

"Quickly, on my shoulders," he said to Callum. "Pull the slats out and see what's out there."

While two of the Festers stood watch by the doorway, Callum jumped onto Roc's shoulders and began tearing out the old vents and handing them down to the other boys. It took only a minute to make a space big enough to climb through. He wriggled onto the sill. They were high up, above the ruined amusement park. Ten feet below, a narrow ledge stretched along a steep wall of concrete.

"There's a ledge but it's not very wide," said Callum.

"Let's get as many of them out as we can," said Roc. "Hold still."

The smaller boys began scaling Roc and Callum's bodies, as if the two of them formed a single tree. When they reached the windowsill, Callum boosted them out into the night. The first boy made a small squawk as he dropped. They managed to set four boys free before the Festers on guard warned of a Squadrone approaching. Callum jumped onto the sill and then turned around to offer Roc his hand, but Roc brushed it aside and pulled himself up before diving through the window. Inside the facility alarms wailed. The two Festers who'd stood guard shouted for Roc to save them but it was too late.

Callum jumped from the windowsill, landing beside Roc. The other Festers had already disappeared into the night. Inside, one of the boys was screaming as if he had been Tasered, and Callum wanted to cover his ears to block out the agonized shrieks. He looked at Roc but Roc ignored the sound as he scanned the terrain.

"Left or right?" asked Callum, swallowing hard.

"They'll send drones for us either way. We'll go straight down."

"But what about the others?"

"They had a head start, and they know where to go. The North Shore is our territory."

As he spoke, Roc began sliding down the slope, scrabbling for a foothold on the cracked concrete. Callum followed, using his hands to slow the speed of his fall. When they reached the bottom of the incline, they teetered on the edge of a thirty-foot drop into darkness. Beneath them, the old amusement park rollercoaster's scaffolding poked up out of the harbor, like a spiderweb etched against the dark water. They could hear a Pally-val taking off from the front of the facility and knew that any minute now they would be spotlighted, an easy target for the Squadrones.

"Use that old roof down there to break your fall," said Roc. Next moment he was gone, launching himself into the inky darkness. Callum shut his eyes and hurled himself off the wall before hesitation could overtake him.

The amusement park roof buckled beneath him and then gave way. As he crashed through two layers of ceiling, he was glad of his circus training. He knew to relax into the fall and trust his instincts. Scrambling out of a pile of shredded canvas and broken timber, he stumbled into the flooded amusement park. A line of clown heads, black water lapping into their open mouths, watched as he scanned the arcade. He stood very still, listening for Roc.

"Roc," he called in a loud whisper. "Where are you?"

He was answered by the roar of descending Pally-vals. Their lights strobed overhead, eerily illuminating the ruined amusement park. Callum took a step forward but the pile of flotsam and jetsam on which he stood shifted beneath his feet and before he knew it, he was up to his waist in pitch-black water. The coldness of it made his skin creep with goose bumps. Gritting his teeth, he waded into the derelict amusement park. He edged his way past fallen spires and coronets, past the rusted Slippery Slide and the shattered Hall of Mirrors, deeper into the ruined Palace of Dreams.

"Slow down, Scab," came Roc's voice. "They'll spot us both if you splash around like that."

The older boy clung with one arm to the frame of a giant cracked mirror as small waves washed against his chest. His face was pale, his body strangely lopsided.

"I landed badly," he said. "You look fine. You must be made of rubber."

"I know how to fall," said Callum. "What happened to you?"

"I hit a pole when I went through the roof. I think my leg's broken."

"What do you want to do? We can't stay here."

Roc didn't answer for a moment. Callum could tell by his breathing that he was in pain.

"Up there, that thing sticking out of the water," said Roc finally. "They won't be able to see us if we climb inside it."

"Okay," said Callum. "Lean on me."

Roc wrapped his arm around Callum's shoulder and Callum staggered under the weight of the bigger boy. Each time they stumbled, Roc's face contorted in agony. They kept to the shadows and slowly, painfully made their way to the cover of a broken amusement ride. As they drew closer, Callum could see that it had once been a merry-go-round.

The Pally-val lights flashed across the water and the dirty mirrors of the merry-go-round sent fragments of light dancing through the ponies. Callum hauled Roc through the maze of horses until he found an ornately carved sled in which they could take shelter. Each time the Pally-vals buzzed low over the amusement park, the boys crouched down, trying to avoid detection.

"We need to move again," said Callum. "We can't do this all night."

Roc winced. "How far?"

"The control booth, in the center of the merry-go-round. The lights won't be able to reach us in there."

Roc groaned as Callum hauled him up the steps and into the black heart of the control booth.

At dawn, a soft light spread across the amusement park. It seeped in under the cover of the merry-go-round and woke Callum. Now that he could see, he realized Roc's left foot was twisted away from his body, as if it were sewn on sideways, and the whole of his leg was mottled and swollen.

When Callum knelt down beside him, Roc opened one bloodshot eye.

"We have to get out of here, Scab. They might send a boat down to scout for us once it's light. If you help me into the water, we can swim for it, and crawl to shore farther north, past the point."

Callum couldn't see Roc swimming more than a few yards, let alone all the way around the rocky shore, but he had no better plan.

"Maybe I can find something to keep us afloat," he said.

He climbed out of the merry-go-round and scanned the amusement park. Everything was awash with a pinkish glow and a crowd of seagulls swooped over the crumpled clown-face entrance. Over by the Ferris wheel, a flotilla of rubbish ebbed against its superstructure. Wedged between the detritus and the wheel was a small platform—a raft. Callum dog-paddled out to the wreckage.

The "raft" was only a series of planks held together by a single crosspiece with a flotation device lashed to the two front corners. Callum scrambled onto it, still clinging to the Ferris wheel for support in case the raft tipped over. He drew a floating branch out of a matted knot of seaweed and driftwood and used it to push the raft away, trying to paddle it toward the merry-go-round. Roc had dragged himself out of the control booth and sat clinging to the leg of a white wooden pony, waiting.

"You'll have to try and swim to the raft. I can't bring it into the merry-go-round," called Callum. "The tide is against me."

Roc looked at the short distance, took a deep breath, and doggedly thrashed his way to the edge of the raft. It rocked wildly as Callum hauled him onto the weathered planks.

"I'll take you around the edge of the harbor," said Callum. "That way you won't have to go far to find Festie. We'll make a splint for your leg, and you can rest there. Then I'm going to cross over to the south side to find my fathers. And Bo. I need to find Bo. Then we'll all try to help the Festers."

Roc lay on his back, his pale face turned to the morning sky.

"You don't understand, Scab. Your fathers . . ."

He breathed deeply for a few minutes and then continued. "Your fathers will betray you or be killed for betraying the Colony. And Bo . . ."

"What? You think Bo will betray me, too? Because you think girls are evil or something? She's not like that."

Roc spoke without opening his eyes. "You're never going to see Bo again. They won't let you near her. She belongs to the old men now."

"I brought her here. I promised I'd help her."

"Isn't a promise you can keep." He seemed to drift into sleep, as if the effort of talking had drained him of all his strength.

Callum began to angle the raft out of the amusement park, using the branch as both a pole and a paddle.

Roc spoke again. "Harbor—full of mines," he said, without opening his eyes. "Try for shore, not harbor."

"I'm trying," snapped Callum. But they were swept into a current and carried into open water.

"I'm not going to make it," said Roc, suddenly opening his eyes.

"Hold on!" cried Callum. Roc was slipping from the raft, his legs trailing in the water.

Callum tried to haul him back but Roc was a dead weight, his hands icy cold, his body limp. The makeshift oar fell overboard and drifted away on the tide. Callum lay across Roc, pinning him to the raft, but he knew he couldn't keep him there for long.

"Help Festers," said Roc. "Festers take old men down. Take down old men—girl belongs to you." Each word taxed him until his strength was gone. He lay limp and exhausted, his eyes closed.

"Don't talk, Roc," said Callum. "Save your strength."

"Go to The Crag," he rasped. "Find Festie. Tell him . . . make Festers strong. Gaias will help. Tell him . . . find Sons of Gaia."

A small wave broke over the raft and Callum was washed into the sea. As he scrabbled back on board, Roc slipped over the side. Callum reached for him but all he saw was the pale glint of Roc's head sinking deep beneath the blue green water.

Callum let out a howl and a lone seagull echoed his cry. He shouted at the wind and clung to the raft as it was swept farther into the harbor. Finally, when his voice grew hoarse, he sat up and scanned the water. He was alone, completely alone and adrift.

Above, the morning sky turned a deeper blue. The raft rocked crazily beneath him, cresting the waves as it drifted, following the tide. Rising from the water, like spiky black sea anemones, were hundreds of mines. The raft bobbed precariously between them, passing into the shadow of a huge broken suspension bridge that had once spanned the harbor from south to north. He stared up at the wreckage. Long cords of steel dangled from it, and Callum realized this was his one chance of survival. Although the center of the bridge had been blown away, the far section joined cleanly with the south shore. Without stopping to think, he started to climb the thick steel cable. It was like shinnying up a tree made of twisted metal. The wind made his sweat cold and his hands grew raw as he clambered upward like a monkey.

At the halfway point, he could see right across the North Shore. In the middle of the harbor was the island Mater Misericordiae, and beyond that, the tall concrete wall that snaked along the southern shore of the harbor, cordoning off the Colony on South Head. And there was the Nekhbet Tower, the morning sun bouncing off its sheer glass walls. It was like a sign. If he returned to the Tower, maybe he could find a clue as to what had happened to his fathers. Somewhere in the old apartment, there had to be evidence of where they had gone, of how he could find them.

When it had all become clear in his mind, he heard the first explosion. A burst of fire and a cloud of black smoke blew out from behind the building. In quick succession, seven other explosions followed. The sides of the Nehkbet Tower exploded outward, sending glass and debris cascading into the city below. Callum put a fist to his mouth to fight back the scream that was swelling inside him as blast after blast rocked the tower. Two small figures, like dolls, leaped from a window, tumbling earthward like wingless birds.

And then Callum fell, too. It was as if all his hopes came crashing down. As the tower fell, he lost his grip on the cable. He dropped down, down into the harbor, the slap of the cold salt water signaling the end of his hopes.

28
Living with Li-Li

"See, there, just south of the Wall?" said Li-Li. "That white building with the lawns reaching down to the water? That's where we're going. That's our home. The Zenana."

Bo pressed her face against the smooth glass of the Pally-val window. The Wall snaked its way across the peninsula to a distant ocean-blue horizon. It sealed off the tip of the South Head of the harbor, making the long wedge of land into another sort of island, with the ruined city pushing up against it. In contrast to the blackened buildings and smudges of umber-colored parkland that made up the city, the land on the peninsula was a patchwork of green gardens and neatly tiled roofs.

Bo turned her gaze to the North Shore, where dark and ragged bushland edged the harbor. Somewhere in that dense tangle, Mr. Pinkwhistle was wandering alone and

Callum was incarcerated. She couldn't bear to think of them, lost and trapped. They had been as constant as her shadow and now she felt weightless without them. Like an old reflex, her hand longed to reach for Callum, to scoop Mr. Pinkwhistle into her arms or snap her fingers for him to follow. She put her hands in her lap and stared at them and then began to flick through the pages of the book that Meera had given her. It was full of stories she had already read but at least it distracted her from her grief.

"Do you have to keep your face in that thing all the time?" asked Li-Li. "Meera may have acted impressed but it's no big deal. It won't change anything for you. It won't save you from anything."

Bo thought to say *It will save me from feeling irritated by your prattle!* but she shut her book and drummed her fingers against its hard blue cover.

"It will be so good to be home," said Li-Li, leaning across Bo so that she too could see the approach to the Colony. She lowered her voice and glanced at the drones piloting the Pally-val. "I don't ever want to go back to Mater Misericordiae. Never ever again."

"You said we were there for our own good," said Bo.

"I say a lot of things because I'm told to say them, not because I believe them," Li-Li said in an angry whisper.

Bo lowered her voice, too. "What did they do to me while I was asleep?"

"Tests. They were testing you."

"But what sort of tests? Did they think I had the plague? What did they do to me?"

Li-Li pulled away from Bo and stared sullenly out the window. "How should I know?" she said.

The Pally-val landed on a helipad at the top of a long, wide avenue and taxied down to the entrance of the Zenana. Two drones and two figures in shroudlike clothes were waiting to escort the girls to a limousine. They were driven down the avenue and onto the grounds of a sprawling sandstone mansion.

Li-Li let out a yelp of pleasure as they passed through the cast-iron gates of the Zenana. "I'm so glad to be back."

She flung open the door of the limousine and jumped out onto the wide green lawn.

Bo hesitated.

"Hurry up, Bo," called Li-Li. "Come and meet everyone." She grabbed Bo by both hands and pulled her out into the sunshine. Bo found it awkward to run in the long skirts that she had been forced to wear, but Li-Li simply hitched them up over her knees, taking the front steps of the house two at a time. She pushed open the double front doors of the Zenana and spun around to face Bo, spreading her arms wide.

"We're home!" she said.

Li-Li led Bo into an open living area where wide, curving windows arced around the walls, providing sweeping views of the harbor. On a creamy white window seat piled high with plush cushions and rugs, more than a dozen small girls were seated. They squealed in unison at the sight of Li-Li.

Bo stood shyly at the entrance to the room as Li-Li rushed from one girl to another, hugging them or picking the little ones up in her arms and covering them with kisses. Bo counted seventeen girls ranging in size from tiny toddlers in fluffy pink tutus to long-limbed ten-year-olds.

Finally, Li-Li turned to look at Bo. She held the smallest child on her hip and for the first time since she had met her, Bo saw Li-Li's expression was open and happy.

"We have another sister. This is Bo," she said, beckoning Bo across the room. "And this little peach I'm holding is Lolly."

"How'd they make her so big?" asked a small blond girl who stood at Li-Li's elbow.

"Serene, can't you think of something nicer to say to Bo?"

"It's all right," said Bo, speaking directly to Serene. "I just grew this way. One day you'll be bigger, too."

"We don't have any big girls here," said Serene solemnly.

"We have Meera," said one of the other children. "And Verity."

"They're not real girls," said Serene, sneering. "They're not even lady-mummies; they're boygies."

"Serene!" said Li-Li. "You know that's not kind."

"But real girls go away and never come back," said Serene.

Li-Li put down Lolly and swept Serene into her arms, tickling her until the small girl squealed and giggled. "I've come back, though. Haven't I?" said Li-Li. "Your Li-Li has come back to you!"

Serene looked at her with distrust. "But no one else has."

Li-Li pursed her lips and dropped Serene onto the silky white lounge. She grabbed Bo by the hand. "Don't listen to the minipin," she said. "Come and see your new home."

Li-Li dragged Bo around the Zenana, showing her one room after another, giving a detailed commentary on the dance room, the dining hall, the indoor and outdoor pools, and the cinema, where a whole wall was taken up by a floor-to-ceiling screen. "Not that there are many movies to watch anymore," said Li-Li. "I've seen all the ones we're allowed to see. They're boring when you've watched them twenty times. But they will be fun to watch again with you. I'll be able to explain everything."

Bo felt a sinking sensation in her stomach. Li-Li spent so much time explaining things yet nothing she said answered the thousand questions that churned inside Bo's mind. When Li-Li showed her the bedroom they would share, Bo shut the door and turned to face her.

"Why won't you explain what happened at Mater Misericordiae? Why do they keep all these girls here at the Zenana, and why are they all so young? Where do they come from? And where do they go? What did Serene mean when she said that big girls don't come back? Why did you come back? What's a boygie? You've explained why you paint your fingernails bright red and why you need to be able to walk around with a book on your head. But you don't explain anything important."

Li-Li shut her eyes and her face grew still. "Can't you

just be happy that we're safe? If you ask me secrets, then I'll have to tell you lies."

That evening, the girls all ate at a long dining table. As the eldest girls, Li-Li and Bo sat at one end while Meera and Verity oversaw proceedings from the other. There were fruits that Bo had never seen before, and sweets and puddings exactly like the ones she had read about in books. As she looked down the table, at the rows of little girls eating daintily from their plates, she was struck by how they all looked like princesses. They wore bright dresses and their faces shone with good health. Their hands were small and neat and perfectly manicured. Bo couldn't help comparing them with the Festers, with their thick manes of matted hair and dirt ingrained in every pore of their bodies.

Meera and Verity looked like queens, their necks laden with gold jewelry and their hair swept into elaborate chignons. Whatever a boygie was, Bo couldn't imagine that a real woman could be more elegantly feminine.

After dinner, they all went into the living room. Bo was amazed at how much the girls laughed and talked. Even the smallest girls emitted a constant stream of chatter. Bo thought of the silent legion of Festers marching through the bush and once again had a sense of the strangeness of her new world.

While Li-Li busily chatted with the smaller girls, Bo retreated to the window seat and gazed out across the harbor to the spot fires on the far North Shore. She was locked in thought when a blast of music began to play from a loudspeaker and all the girls let out a shout of excitement. Some of them began to jump around, dancing and laughing as the music grew louder. Bo turned to watch as Li-Li tried to organize the smallest girls into rows but as soon as her back was turned each child spun away, caught up in the music and her own chaotic whirl. The song they danced to was nothing like the wild cacophony of the Festers. It was high and sweet, full of rhythms and tones that Bo had never heard before. It stirred a longing inside her that made her look away from the color of the dancing girls and back to the dark North Shore. Callum would love this music, this moment when the room was filled with sound and movement. She thought of the way he had danced and twirled before the Festers' bonfire and tried to imagine him among the whirling young girls. Even though he had grown up with Colony Men, he hadn't known this place existed. Why weren't Colony boys allowed in the Zenana?

As if Li-Li could see Bo's thoughts wandering into dangerous territory, she grabbed her hands and dragged her to her feet. The little girls danced around her, waving their arms in the air. "Dance with us, Bo. Dance," they shouted as the music grew louder and the whole room swelled with sound. Li-Li put her hand on Bo's shoulder and bumped her with her hip, deliberately and in time to the music. Bo caught her breath. An unnameable feeling bubbled inside her the same way it had when she danced with the Festers, but this time it made her laugh. For the first time in her life, she felt graceful, as if when Li-Li led her in the dance, her body knew exactly how to move. A thin sheen of sweat covered her skin but she felt clean and unburdened. When Lolly stretched her hands out, Bo swept the tiny pink-and-white girl into her arms and whirled her about in the air so the child shrieked with excitement.

When the music subsided, all the girls collapsed on the floor in fits of giggles. "You make fun," said Lolly. She wrapped her arms tightly around Bo's neck and covered her face with kisses. "I love you, big Bo. You love me, too?" Bo stroked Lolly's face and looked into her eyes. No one had ever told Bo they loved her and yet this tiny girl who barely knew her said it so freely. Without understanding what instinct possessed her, Bo kissed the little girl on the cheek and cuddled her close. "I love you, too, little Lolly."

Early the next morning, Bo woke to find a child standing beside her bed, holding a breakfast tray. She rubbed her eyes and sat up. Li-Li was already awake and sitting propped up by fluffy pillows, sipping a steaming cup of tea.

"Thank you," said Bo, reaching for her cup.

"You don't have to thank him," said Li-Li. "It's his job."

Bo looked at the child and her heart leaped in her chest. "Flakie?" But he looked so different. His hair had been shorn within an inch of his scalp and his face was scrubbed clean. He wore a long-sleeved white uniform with small gold buttons. He didn't look at Bo when she spoke to him but kept staring straight ahead, a fixed smile upon his face.

Bo took the tray and shoved it onto the bedside table. She grabbed him by both arms and gripped him hard.

"Flakie, it is you, isn't it? How did you get here? Where are Callum and Roc and the other boys? What have they done with them?"

Flakie kept smiling fixedly, his eyes vacant.

"What's wrong with him?" asked Bo, turning to Li-Li. "Why is he like this?"

"That's how he's supposed to be," said Li-Li. "That's what I mean. Boys are dumb. I can't see what you like about them. They're all so dopey."

"This isn't normal," said Bo. "Something's happened to him. He wasn't like this before."

"They've trained him. He's meant to be like that. We're not allowed to have the older boys or drones look after us, or even look at us, so they send us these stupid little boys."

"Flakie," said Bo, shaking him by his shoulders. "Flakie, wake up," she shouted.

At that moment, Meera came into the bedroom. She snapped her fingers at Flakie and he trotted over to her side.

"That's enough, Bo. You're not allowed to touch the servants."

"He's not a servant!" shouted Bo. "He's one of the Festers. I want to see the other Festers. What have you done with them?"

Meera pushed Flakie out into the hallway and glared at Bo. "There are no such things as Festers. You mustn't talk about them. You'll frighten the other girls with your stories. If you keep talking like this, we'll have to send you back to Mater Misericordiae."

Li-Li jumped up and put her arms around Bo. "Bo was having a bad dream and the boy gave her a fright, Meera. She must have been dreaming about those silly old Festery things, really, truly. She was making piggy noises in her sleep, so that means she was having bad dreams, doesn't it? That boy didn't knock when he came in. He scared us and Bo woke up frightened. That's all that happened."

Li-Li turned to Bo and squeezed her cheeks. "It's all right now, Bosey-Wosey. It was all a bad dream and now you're back in the real world, safe and sound."

As soon as Meera had pulled the door shut, Bo slapped Li-Li's hands away.

"Why are you lying?"

Li-Li looked at her coldly. "To protect you, of course. Though I don't know why I bother." She stood up and straightened her nightgown. "For someone so smart, you can be incredibly stupid. Can't you see you put everyone at risk, not least that poor, dumb drone of a boy?"

"What are they going to do to Flakie? Will they punish him?"

"You don't need to worry about what they do to the boys. Don't you understand? We're the ones that have to be careful. We're the ones that they want to hurt."

29
Hunting Down a Dream

Callum lay for hours in the baking sun. Somehow he had managed to make it to shore but there was no strength left in his body by the time he crawled onto a rock beyond the point. As the sun began to set, he staggered into the bush. Scrambling up the trunk of a Moreton Bay fig tree, he found a comfortable resting place in its nexus of branches. Darkness settled over the North Shore and he discovered he wasn't the only one seeking shelter in the tree. A flapping legion of black creatures wheeled out into the night sky, shrieking to each other until he had to cover his ears. It was the stuff of nightmares. After hours in the cold harbor, and the long, hot afternoon trudging through the bush, his body ached for rest. Despite the traffic of bats, he fell into an exhausted sleep.

An hour before dawn he woke, cramped and stiff, to

find the air was sharp with the scent of fires. A pall of smoke hung over the south shore as the Nehkbet Tower continued to burn. Callum turned his back on it and headed north. Late in the afternoon, when he'd almost given up hope, he wandered into an abandoned garden full of gnarled fruit trees. Plump peaches hung from the branches. Callum reached up to pick one, but something sharp hit the back of his hand.

"Ouch!" he yelled.

"Hey, Scab," shouted Festie, jumping out from between the fruit trees, slingshot in hand. "These ones been baited. You'd be done like Blister if you ate any. How did you get here? Did the Festers escape? Did Roc get away too?"

"Maybe a couple of others are free. But not Roc," said Callum, shutting his eyes and remembering the chaos of the night of the breakout.

"Not Roc," echoed Festie, his voice heavy with disappointment.

Callum couldn't look at him. He hung his head in silence.

Festie sighed. "Well, you better come and eat something, then. I got a fire and some crickets on the coals. C'mon, mate. You look done in."

On a craggy rise overlooking an inlet, Festie had built a small camp. "I figured the houses weren't safe for a while. Too many Squadrones and baiters around."

Callum was amazed to see two figures in the camp, sitting in the shade of a peppercorn tree. Bug had a long piece of twine tied around his waist and secured to a branch. Crouched beside him, bobbing from foot to foot, stood Mr. Pinkwhistle.

"He's peculiar, that critter," said Festie. "Seems to have some sort of programming that protects kids. Watch this."

As soon as Festie untied Bug, the toddler jumped up and ran toward the fire with a squeal of excitement. Mr. Pinkwhistle was between the child and the flames in a flash, herding the little boy away from the fire and back to the shade of the peppercorn tree, as if the boy were a sheep to be corralled.

"See?" said Festie. "Weird, eh?"

"Bo probably programmed him to do that," said Callum. "Where is Bo?"

Callum put his face in his hands. "They took her away."

"Her?"

They sat by the fire roasting crickets and cicadas while Callum told Festie everything that had happened since the raid. When he got to the part where Bo was taken away from them, Festie shook his head in disbelief.

"Everything goes to pieces when there are girls."

"How do you know? Have you ever met a girl?"

"Roc said they were like poison, that they ruined everything. He said if boys could work together and not worry about girls, we could make a better world."

Callum swallowed hard, trying not to think about that moment when Roc had slipped from the raft and disappeared beneath the waves. "Roc said to tell you to grow the Festers again."

"Me?" asked Festie, surprised.

"Before he died, he said you have to make them strong."

Festie looked into the fire and poked at the embers. For a long while, he was silent. Finally, he said, "And you, Scab?"

"I need to get into South Head. My dads might be there. They worked for the Colony and now that the Nehkbet Tower is gone . . ."

"Gone? The Gaias must have done that. It should have been the Festers that took it down."

"The Gaias? Roc said something about them, too. He said you should find the Sons of Gaia."

"I'm not going near that lot. Not even for Roc's sake."

"Who are they?"

"A pack of devils ready to slit your throat or sell your soul. Roc bought explosives and weapons from them. We used to rule all the tunnels under the city until they came along. Roc didn't want to believe it, but I think the Gaias slunk around our territory, sniped our boys, sold us rubbish, tricked us at every turn."

Callum recalled the eerie voices that had called out to him and Bo in the flooded subway.

"But Roc trusted them."

"Roc was a great leader. But he only saw one side of things."

"Do you think everything he said about the Colony was true?"

"I know what I've seen," said Festie. "You've seen it, too."

Callum shuddered at the memory of the ROT facility. "All I want is to find my fathers and then find Bo so we can be a family. We don't need the Colony, we just need each other."

"You know," said Festie, "I've heard you can make kids with girls and you don't even need a lab to do it."

Festie drew Bug onto his lap and fed the little boy a cicada.

"That's not why I want to find her," said Callum. "If we can find my dads, too, we could all run away."

"You'll never get into the Colony," said Festie. "They'll think you're a Fester and harmonize you before you can open your mouth."

"Then I'll sneak in. Once I'm over the Wall, at least I'll have a chance."

"The only ones that can help you break into South Head are the Gaias. If you're cunning, cunning as a cockroach, you might get them to take you into the tunnels that they've been making under the Wall. It's the only way. That or flying."

Festie reached inside his shirt and pulled out a long, crumpled piece of white fabric. Unfurled, the material revealed itself as a banner. In the center was a painting of a black flower exactly like the one Callum had seen on the notepaper in his fathers' apartment.

"You take this. Tie it to a long stick and make sure you carry it with you. Then the Gaias will know that you're there for business. But watch your back—they're snakes."

"What about you, Festie? Don't you want to use it? Aren't you going to do what Roc wanted?"

"No, I was never cut out to be a Disease. That was Roc's dream. Not mine."

He tickled Bug under the chin. "I'll take care of this one until he's growed bigger. Then we'll be a team and we'll go find other littlies to take care of. Make ourselves our own little tribe. I want to make things grow, not kill them. That's my dream. You, Scab, sounds like you've got a bigger dream to hunt."

Festie got to his feet and crossed to a heap of bark and sticks. From inside he drew out Bo's string bag and then he scooped up Mr. Pinkwhistle and offered both the bag and the roboraptor to Callum.

"Reckon you'll be needing these," he said.

30
Ripeness

Bo threw the book she'd been reading over the side of her chair. Was this what "boredom" felt like? At Tjukurpa Piti there had always been something to fix or something to hunt. The Zenana was full of entertainments, but after a few days they had lost their attraction and Bo couldn't contain her restlessness.

Across the harbor, somewhere on the North Shore, the ruins of an old building were on fire. Bo wondered if a Fester had started it. She wished she was there, sitting by a bonfire with the Festers. Her gaze drifted across the water to Mater Misericordiae and she felt a tiny shiver course through her. She touched her hips gently, checking to see if the tenderness in her groin had subsided.

There was a flurry of excited calls from the hallway. "Bo, Bo, the husbands are coming tonight," called Serene.

"Meera and Verity are going to do our nails. Come and make pretty."

Bo could see the girls gathering on the tiered steps of the adjoining lounge room, while Verity knelt before them, carefully decorating each of their tiny toenails with flowers and hearts.

Li-Li came to the door of the viewing room and beckoned Bo.

"Why don't you come and join us? Why do you always have to make yourself separate?"

"I'm not making myself separate. I'm thinking."

"Well, stop it. It will only get us into trouble."

Bo sighed. "It won't get you into trouble, Li-Li."

"Wake up, Bo. This could be our last season here. We should make the most of it. They're going to take both of us away soon, back to Mater Misericordiae. As soon as we're ripe enough."

"You said you never wanted to go there again. And what do you mean, ripe enough? You never explain anything."

Li-Li looked at the floor. "That's because I never mean anything," she said. She turned away and started to climb up the stairs, back to the circular mezzanine.

Bo ran after her and grabbed her arm. "Li-Li, what is going to happen to us? And if you don't know, how can you live like this? Not knowing and having them in control of everything you do."

Li-Li grew limp. She stretched her arms around Bo's neck and clung to her, resting her head on Bo's shoulder. "I can't tell you," she whispered into Bo's ear. "Not here, not now."

214

Late in the day, as dusk settled over the gardens, the girls assembled in the main lounge. Bo ran her hand down her thigh, feeling the smooth, silky fabric against her skin. In honor of the visit of the husbands, all the girls were dressed in new outfits. Each girl wore a different color. Bo's outfit was turquoise with a fine silver thread running through the weave. Li-Li's was magenta. Serene wore blue and Lolly was in baby pink. Gathered together, they looked like a flock of beautiful birds.

When the husbands arrived, Bo was a little disappointed. They were seven ordinary men, older than most of the drones she had seen but younger than Mollie Green. Bo wondered whose husbands they were meant to be, as they brought no women with them. Nor did any of them seem very interested in the girls. They talked among themselves as Verity and Meera offered them trays of food and drink. Every now and then they would ask a girl to join them. The girl would stand patiently beside the man who had asked for her company until Verity told her to go back to her seat.

Li-Li took Bo by the hand. "I'd better introduce you," she said, gloomily. "Verity said I had to."

She led Bo over to a small group of men who stood near the entrance to the terrace.

"This is Bo," said Li-Li. "She's new. A foundling. She was in the wilderness but now she's with us. She's very clever. Cleverer than me but not too clever."

Bo laughed and Li-Li elbowed her sharply.

One of the men put his finger on Li-Li's cheek. "There's no one in the Zenana as clever as you, Li-Li. Not even Verity or Meera. Some would say you're too clever for your own good."

Li-Li suppressed a little snort of annoyance. "This is Hackett," she said.

Hackett was taller than the other men. His black hair was smoothly combed and slicked back. He leaned down to talk to Bo, his mouth close to her ear, and his breath was warm and minty against her cheek.

"Welcome to the Zenana, Bo. I want you to know that if there is anything I can help you with, you only have to ask. Perhaps I could come a little earlier next week and we could walk around the garden together. Get to know each other. I want you to be happy here."

Bo liked the way he spoke to her, as if she were his equal. She looked up into his broad, handsome face and smiled.

"I'd like that," said Bo. "It's very dull here, being cooped up all the time." Then she turned to see that Li-Li had grown pale, her eyes glittering.

"Are you all right?" she asked, putting one arm around Li-Li. "You look faint."

"I don't feel very well. Will you help me upstairs?"

In their bedroom, Li-Li drew the curtains and pushed a chair against the door. Then she climbed into bed and put her arms out for Bo to join her. When they were nestled snugly under the blankets, Li-Li cupped her hands around Bo's ear and began to whisper in a low, raspy voice. Bo realized she was crying.

"Promise me you won't go anywhere with Hackett?"
"Why?"

"Because he'll hurt you, the way he hurt me. I had to

go to Mater Misericordiae because of him. He made me bleed. Meera thought I had my period but it was Hackett's fault. I wasn't ready but he tried to . . . to make me ripe."

"You're doing it again. Saying things that make no sense. What do you mean?"

Li-Li took a deep breath and spoke softly. "When we get older, we start to bleed. It happens to all girls. We bleed every month. That's when we're ripe. That's when they'll take us back to the island. We'll have to stay there while they harvest us."

"Harvest?"

"Alethea told me that girls have over four hundred thousand eggs inside them. Eggs to make babies. Once a month, we bleed, which is a sign that the eggs haven't made a baby. They need seeds from boys to hatch. In our lives, only four or five hundred of our eggs will ripen properly. At Mater Misericordiae they give you medicine to help make lots of eggs come out every month, not just one. And they keep them safe in freezers to make babies with later. Some girls get sick from the drugs and then they never come back to the Colony. And most girls, not pretty girls, they stay and incubate babies. Nearly all of the babies are grown in glass jars but special babies are grown inside the incubator girls for a while. Those precious ones, the girl babies and chosen boys, are put inside the incubator girls for a few months. Then they're cut out again and put in glass boxes until they're fully cooked. And then the brewers put more babies in the incubator girls. So they cook tiny babies and are cut open over and over again. It's horrible."

Bo felt dizzy.

"Why don't they leave the babies in the girls until they're ready to be born? Boys and girls."

"Because they're running out of time. They need more girls and more babies. That's why they feed us so well and take care of us. They want us to be healthy breeders."

"I don't understand. Why don't they just make all the babies inside glass boxes? Why do the girls have to incubate them?"

"Only the boy babies grow well under glass. Things always go wrong with the girl babies if they're not inside a mother. And even the boy babies in the glass boxes, sometimes they don't work either."

"Is that where the Festers came from? The glass boxes instead of the mothers?"

"I think they use animal eggs to make some boys. Or maybe the Festers were ones that didn't cook fully."

"They looked pretty cooked to me."

"I don't know!" said Li-Li, her whispering growing louder. "I don't know everything. All I do know is that the mothers can only incubate a few babies each year so they keep you on the Island forever. Incubating and incubating forever and ever until you die. That's why I went with Hackett. I thought he would want me to be his wife. The pretty girls are chosen by the husbands. They don't have to die. I let Hackett hurt me because I thought he'd help me get back from the Island when I grew up. Once they have all your eggs, you can come back to the Colony and get married, if one of the men wants you. I don't want to be like my mother and die on the Island."

"Your mother?"

Li-Li rolled away from Bo and covered her face with her hands.

"They lied to her. They told her the Island was a safe place for women. We sailed into the harbor together. She thought we would find a home here, but she was wrong. They brought me to the Zenana and took her away. When I went to Mater Misericordiae I thought I'd find her, but I found the truth. The horrible truth."

"We have to get out of here, Li-Li," said Bo, sitting up.

Li-Li pulled her back down under the covers. "Shhh," she said, stroking Bo's face and pulling the coverlet up over their heads. "They can hear everything we say, unless we're careful. Bad girls disappear, the way my mother did. That's why we have to be nice to everyone, Bo. Girls have to be nice to try and get a husband. That's why the husbands come every week. They watch you and wait and if you're nice enough, they'll help you later."

It was hot and fetid beneath the covers but Bo couldn't push them back until she had all the answers.

"Like Hackett? Do you think he'll help you?"

"Maybe I wasn't nice enough," said Li-Li, despondently. "Maybe if I'm nice to one of the other husbands, they'll want me."

"I'm not 'nice' at all, Li-Li. I don't want to marry someone like Hackett, and I don't want to be one of their incubators either."

"Neither do I!" sobbed Li-Li. "But better to marry than to incubate forever. That's what Meera says." She wept hot, angry tears that spilled onto Bo's shoulder.

"But Meera and Verity. Why do they get to look after all the girls and not die on Mater Misericordiae?"

"They're boygies—you know, shemales. They aren't good for breeding but they make the Colony work."

"I don't know what that means. But I do know one thing. You won't go back to Mater Misericordiae. Neither will I. We're going away," said Bo firmly.

Li-Li choked back her tears, almost as if she were laughing.

"Oh Bo, don't you understand! Once you turn into a woman, you won't be able to live with the Festers. You could only do that because they didn't know what you were. There is nowhere to go, nowhere safe for women."

Bo was quiet. "Even if the world is dangerous, I can make my way in it. I don't need the Zenana. I can make my own home. I had one before, I will have one again."

"My mother had a home, too, an island where I was born, far to the north."

"Was that the magic faraway place you told Serene about in your story?"

"I made some of that up. I can't remember very much about it, I was so small. I don't even know what it was called. It feels like a dream from an imaginary life. But I know there were other women there, and I think we were happy. Then one day, when we were out at sea, there was a storm. The island disappeared. We were swept away and drifted for weeks until we sailed through the Heads, into Vulture's Gate."

Bo pulled Li-Li's head onto her shoulder and stroked her silky hair. "Are you sure the island was destroyed in the storm? I mean, what if it's still there? A place where you can grow into a woman and not be afraid? Where there are so many women that it's normal?"

Li-Li was silent for a long time. "How would we get there?"

"Somehow," said Bo, "we'll find a way."

31
Sons of Gaia

It took Callum three days to reach the middle harbor where the Gaias had their base. Festie had explained that the Sons of Gaia lived in a tower of dead wood, an aerie built on the side of a precipice. In places the bush was so thick that Callum had to carry Mr. Pinkwhistle in the string bag, for fear he would lose him in the thorny black-berries. Without coordinates, he could only rely on instinct.

He spotted the aerie long before he reached it. Remembering Festie's instructions, he unfurled the white banner with the black flower and secured it to a stick. Then he crawled along rocky waterways and scrambled through dense undergrowth until the banner looked limp and ragged and his knees were bloody with gashes. As he drew closer, he saw guards scattered through the bush. A

222

hundred Sons of Gaia watched silently from beneath wide-brimmed bark hats as Callum made his way to the base of the aerie. No one spoke, no one questioned his mission.

A tall, skinny man in khaki shorts stepped forward as Callum approached. His legs were like the knotty roots of an old tree and his eyes were sunken in his leathery face.

"You are not the leader of the Festers. State your name and business."

"Callum Caravaggio. Roc is dead. I am the new leader of the Festers."

Callum thought his voice sounded odd, too childlike. They'd never believe him. Festie had made him recite the announcement but when it came out of his mouth here, at the base of the Gaias' stronghold, it sounded tinny and unbelievable.

The man gestured for Callum to climb the ladder. He followed him up a winding flight of stairs. At the top was a tiny room looking out over the harbor. It was full of bird droppings, and pigeons roosted on the windowsills. As Callum stepped over the threshold, he thought of Bo, of how terrifying this would be for her. Suddenly, he realized he, too, was afraid.

Another Son of Gaia stood by the window. Like the man with the ropy legs, he was dressed in a khaki-colored shirt and very short shorts. His head was smooth and shiny, though his chin was covered with a bushy beard.

"Welcome, Callum Caravaggio. I am Quoll and this is Quokka," he said, gesturing to the man who had led Callum up the ladders. "We are the eldest Children of Gaia in this aerie."

"I want to talk to Gaia. He's your leader, isn't he?"

The men laughed and indicated for him to sit down, but Callum chose to stand.

"She. Gaia is our mother."

Callum was bewildered. "I don't get it," he said.

Quokka and Quoll looked at one another and shook their heads. "Gaia is your mother also. She is the mother of all the sons of men. Gaia isn't a woman. She is the planet Earth. And as you know, she has been ill. She is trying to heal herself and we, as her loyal sons, are helping her."

"Helping her?"

"By assisting her to rid herself of the most noxious creatures on the planet, the creatures she has been trying to divest herself of for generations." Quokka leaned forward. "The sons of men. We have a mission to eradicate every last human. When we are gone, the earth's balance will be restored."

It took a moment for Callum to make sense of what Quokka had said. "You're the ones who bait the Festers." In his mind's eye, he could see Bo walking across a courtyard with Blister's body in her arms.

"We do not intend to poison all the Festers. Not while they are of use to us. Only the strays. If some of the Festers fall victim to the baits, this is because Gaia wills it. The Festers only exist because Gaia wishes them to assist in her endgame."

"Roc said you could help us," said Callum. His head was throbbing. The more he heard, the less he understood.

"We work in mysterious ways," said Quoll, smiling at

Callum's confusion. "The Festers are nimble and reckless. Their hatred of the Colony served us well. But we heard news of the Festers' destruction. Without your tribe, what can you offer?"

"It's true. There aren't many of us left. Right now, there's only me. But I know that you're digging under the south Wall and I want to help. I'm good in small places. I can wriggle in anywhere. And I have this."

He lifted Mr. Pinkwhistle out of Bo's string bag and set him on the floor of the attic.

Quoll and Quokka stepped back warily. "This is the technology of the Colony. Merely a toy from the before times."

"No, he's better than any toy. He has all sorts of sensors that can help you underground," said Callum. "GPSs don't work down there, do they? But Mr. P has a muon detector and I know how to work it. Me and Mr. P could be useful to you."

The men put their heads together and whispered while Callum waited. The aerie swayed slightly as another man climbed up the ladder and into the tiny attic.

Quokka looked up. "Koala, you have finished?"

"I have fulfilled the promise. Nehkbet Tower is destroyed," he said. He pushed past Callum and set a tray of food and tiny cups of steaming liquid on the floor. Like the other men, he had a shiny bald head but his beard was thick and reddish. When he turned around, Callum felt an electric shock of recognition.

"Rusty! Dad!" cried Callum, flinging his arms around his father.

"Callum?"

No one spoke. Gently, Rusty pushed Callum away and bent down to look into his face. "I thought you were dead, kiddo."

"You know this Fester?" asked Quoll, his voice tinged with disapproval.

Rusty took a step back from Callum. "A Fester? Callum, a Fester?" He fell to his knees in front of Callum and grabbed him by both arms. "You haven't eaten any fruit from the trees on the way here, have you?"

Callum stepped away in horror. "You're the one that lays the baits?" He stumbled across the aerie and picked up Mr. Pinkwhistle, clinging to him. Sensing Callum's distress, Mr. Pinkwhistle mewled and his eyes glowed a soft pink. "Where's Ruff?" asked Callum, dreading the answer. "Where's my other dad?"

Rusty turned to Quoll and Quokka.

"In my former life, this child was my son," he said.

"We do not propagate ourselves. We are the last ones, Koala."

"I chose him before I understood Gaia. I need to speak with him alone. To explain the faith."

Callum's fists were clenched as Quoll and Quokka deliberated. Finally, Quoll spoke.

"There is only one path. There is only one solution. This boy has been sent to help the Mother. He is no longer your son. He is the brother of Roc and the last of the Festers. You may educate him in the ways of the faith but he is not to leave the aerie."

Quoll and Quokka climbed down the rickety ladder,

leaving him alone with Rusty. Night was falling, a silky darkness descending over the bush.

Rusty stretched his arms out to Callum. For a split second, Callum hesitated. Then all his resistance crumbled and he fell into his father's open arms. The tears came thick and fast. He cried so hard his voice grew hoarse with sobbing. And all the while, Rusty stroked his head gently and said his name, over and over again. They sat beneath the roosting birds and Rusty cradled Callum in his arms, as if he were small again. Finally, when Callum's tears had subsided and he lay limp and exhausted against his father's chest, Rusty spoke. "I never thought I'd see you again."

"I always knew I'd find you," said Callum. "Even if it took forever."

"You got that from Ruff," said Rusty. "Stubborn and loyal to the end. He didn't want to leave the west. He was convinced we'd find you. We searched everywhere and circled back to the site of the Refuge time and again. We left a message on Peggy for you and buried her in a box."

"I know," said Callum. "I found it."

Ruff shook his head in disbelief and hugged Callum tighter. "I'm sorry, Callum. I'm so sorry. I thought you were dead. I thought leaving the iPenguin would help Ruff let go. But he insisted we stay another week. We'd already fought off one band of Outstationers and I knew more would come. The next day, they did."

Rusty's eyes grew misty. "The mongrels murdered Ruff. It was all I could do to get away."

For a long moment, Rusty and Callum were silent, grief consuming them both.

"Ruff would be so proud of you, Callum. How on earth did you cross the entire country all by yourself?"

Callum sniffed deeply. "I wasn't alone." The whole story came out, from his time in the circus to meeting Bo and their journey across the continent. Rusty listened patiently, the way he'd always listened to Callum, taking in every word and letting Callum talk until there was nothing left unsaid.

"So you're not really a Fester, then?"

"I don't know. Are you really a Son of Gaia?"

"Absolutely."

"Then, if you're a Son of Gaia," Callum said slowly, "that means I'm a Grandson of Gaia, doesn't it?"

"It doesn't work like that. When you disappeared and Outstationers killed Ruff, I realized we'd made a mistake."

"I was a mistake?"

"Not you. Not Ruff. But everything else—the Colony, the world of men, the endless struggle. I realized there's only one path. One solution."

Callum felt his head was going to explode.

"Like what those crazy old men said? You think everyone is bad? What about the girls? Roc said there are other girls like Bo. If we tell them about the girls, they'll have to think differently. They'll want to save them, won't they?"

"We know about the girls. The girls are part of the problem, not the solution. That's why the Colony has to be destroyed. What they're doing is wrong, Callum. The earth doesn't need girls. Gaia needs liberation from mankind."

Callum sat up and held Rusty's face in his hands. He had to make him see things differently. "Maybe the girls are coming back 'cause Gaia wants them back. I mean, if you think Gaia is a girl, then they can't be all bad."

"I know it's difficult for you to accept, Callum, but I believe in this. I believe the Sons of Gaia have found the true path. I'm not your father anymore, but you and I can work together, like brothers, to make the dream of Gaia a reality."

"You want me to lay bombs? You want me to kill people? Like a Fester?"

"No, like a true Son of Gaia. Not for your own ends, not out of rage but out of love. I took the name of Koala because the koala has been lost to Gaia because of the pestilence of men. Each of us takes a name to symbolize Gaia's grief. It's an act of love. Everything we do is for love."

Callum looked away. Rusty took his hand and held it tightly, and Callum could feel his father's earnest longing. He shut his eyes, trying to block out the sensation.

"You understand, don't you?" asked Rusty.

Callum stood up and crossed over to the window. All along the cliff face, the Sons of Gaia were gathered around small campfires. Beyond, the middle harbor glistened as the moon rose up above the ragged bush. He had traveled so far to be here, to be in this strange, lonely aerie with the last of his fathers.

"I understand," he said.

32
Caged Birds

Two days after the husbands had visited, Li-Li woke Bo early. It was still dark outside but the Zenana was already starting to come to life. "I think you're in trouble," said Li-Li.

"Why?"

"They almost never let us out of the Zenana. Now Hackett has said we're allowed to go to Lady Bay, because you complained about being cooped up. We're only allowed to go there once a year and we've already had our visit. Because of you, we're going again."

"Then why am I in trouble? I'd think everyone would be pleased."

"They are. But Hackett will tell you he did this for you. And ask for something in return."

Bo climbed out of bed and looked out the window at

the dark harbor. Before Hackett could ask anything of her, she had to escape.

Before dawn, Meera and Verity had gotten the girls up and prepared everything for their excursion. Each child was dressed in a close fitting neck-to-knee garment and then draped in long black robes. In the early morning they boarded a small bus with darkened windows. Lolly could barely contain her excitement. She climbed onto Bo's lap, struggling with her heavy robes, and pressed her face against the window, pointing at everything from the front gate to the Squadrones marching down the street in their drab khaki uniforms, as if she had never seen anything so exciting, as if she were a bird being set free from her cage.

The bus stopped at the top of a pathway on the only piece of land left on the South Head not crowded with houses. Bo could see a track was cut into the harbor side of the rocky peninsula. Meera and Verity organized the girls into pairs and they walked in a line to the beach. Thick scrub towered above them on one side, a high stone wall on the other. Eucalyptus cast long shadows across the path. Bo looked longingly into the reserve, wishing Festers were hiding in the bush, imagining they would come out to rescue her.

Two groups of Squadrones accompanied them, one behind and one ahead. Their black boots sounded loudly on the stone path and they stared across the top of the girls' heads, their gaze fixed and eyes glassy. They acted as if they had blinders on, as if the girls were a herd of sheep rather than a group of children.

It didn't take long to reach a weathered flight of stairs

that led down to the shore. Meera instructed the Squadrones to wait and the girls were allowed to walk down the stairs alone. An ancient sign lay in the grass on the side of the path.

"What does it say, Bo?" whispered Serene.

"Lady Bay Beach—nudity permitted on beach only," said Bo, pushing back a clump of native grass to see the words carved into the timber.

"What's a nudity?"

"It's not a thing. It means you're allowed to take your clothes off."

Serene giggled, scandalized. "I never knew it said *that!*"

Even at low tide there was only a tiny strip of beach left as the harbor waters lapped against the shore, trying to reclaim the peninsula. The girls disrobed, leaving their heavy overclothes on the flat rocks that edged the beach while Meera and Verity fussed over them, forcing them all to put on bonnets with wide brims, which were then tied snugly beneath their chins.

"We've only got an hour or two before the tide comes in," said Meera. "But you girls can build sandcastles and swim in the sea. Verity and I have a picnic. We're going to have a lovely morning."

Bo looked across the measly strip of sand. Lady Bay Beach was a small, protected cove with a chain-link fence sealing it off from the harbor. Behind them, the rock face rose like a prison wall. She sighed and sat down in the sand beside Li-Li.

Obediently, all the girls began molding sandcastles,

drawing little pathways from one construction to the next. Li-Li helped some of the smaller girls build while Bo lay down beside Lolly and watched the tiny girl make lumpy mounds and poke her fingers into them. Lolly lined up a row of seashells and showed Bo how they were the windows of her fairy sandcastle. Then she took her baby doll down to the shore and dipped its feet in the water. Immediately, Verity was by her side, hovering over Lolly as if she were about to fall on her face and drown. Lolly slapped the woman's hands away in frustration.

"Can we take off these outfits?" Bo asked Meera, tugging at the close-fitting bodysuit.

Meera stopped handing out cupcakes and frowned. "We don't want you to get sunburned. And do keep your hat on, Bo. You don't want the sun to freckle that pretty face."

Bo laughed. She thought of all the hours she had spent hunting, squinting into the desert sun, with burning light washing across her body. And she thought, with a pang, of the afternoon at the water hole with Callum, the silky water against their skin and how lightly his body had floated in her arms. She walked down to the water's edge where white waves lapped against the shore. The blue green water felt cool as it washed over her feet but when she waded in deeper, the bodysuit clung to her calves.

Serene wandered in to stand beside her. "Wouldn't it be nice to take these clothes off and really swim?" said Bo.

"We always swim in our bodysuits," said Serene.

"What do you think would happen if we took them off?"

"I don't know."

"Let's find out," said Bo. Quickly, she peeled off the bodysuit, stomping down on the yellow fabric until it looked like a flimsy jellyfish beneath the water. Serene giggled and peeled hers off as well, flinging it into the shallows where it floated like a dead creature. It took a moment for Verity and Meera to realize that Bo and Serene were now completely naked.

"Bo! Serene! Put your suits back on this instant," shouted Verity.

"Can you swim?" Bo asked Serene.

"Yes."

"Then let's go!" Bo dived under the cool water and felt the thrill of it washing across her bare skin. Quickly, she freestyled out to the chain-link fence that enclosed the bay. Serene followed and they climbed onto the thick steel cable that stretched across the top of the chain-link fence, sitting like two mermaids with the wide harbor behind them.

On the beach, Verity and Meera began shouting for them to return. The other girls playing in the sand looked up in astonishment. Li-Li began to laugh and in the next instant, she, too, stripped off her bodysuit. She ran past the women, dived into the water, and swam out to join Bo and Serene. Meanwhile, on the beach, all the girls began shedding their suits like second skins and running down to the water's edge, squealing with excitement, while Meera and Verity ran among them, trying to force the littlest girls back into their hats and bodysuits, all to no avail. As soon as they dressed one, another peeled off her clothes and ran shouting into the sea. Soon, all the girls were in the water, splashing each other and shrieking in shrill delight.

Li-Li pulled herself up onto the steel cable and laughed. "I've never swum nude before. It's delicious."

"The sign said we could be naked on the beach, didn't it, Bo?" said Serene. She combed one hand through her blond hair and flicked it over her bare shoulder.

Li-Li laughed again, a low chuckle that made Bo want to hoot with laughter as well.

"Look at all those Squadrones up on the rocks," said Li-Li. "They don't know where to look or what to do. You've really started something."

Bo scanned the harbor and the rocky shore. "How far is it across the Heads?" she asked.

"Too far to swim, if that's what you're thinking."

"And what lies beyond the tip of the peninsula?"

Li-Li followed her gaze to the end of South Head. "The wide, wide ocean. Thousands of miles of open sea." She said it with such longing that Bo took her hand and held it tightly.

They sat on the cable watching the girls splash wildly in the shallows while Meera and Verity shouted in exasperation and hauled the children, one by one, onto the shore.

"We should swim in soon," said Serene, starting to look anxious. "We'll all be punished with the Black Box."

"The Black Box?" said Bo.

"There are two upstairs," said Li-Li. "They put you in them when you're naughty. But they're really nothing more than dark cupboards. The little ones hate it and cry for hours but I don't care. They won't hurt us physically because they want to keep our bodies intact for Mater Misericordiae."

"We'll never be allowed to come back to Lady Bay again, either," said Serene.

"Don't worry. Bo and I won't be with you much longer," said Li-Li bitterly. "Once they've got rid of us troublemakers, they'll bring you back here again."

"But it won't be the same without you! I don't want anything to change."

"Things can change for the better," said Bo. "One day, we might all be free to do as we please."

"One day," sighed Serene. "Everything is one day too far away."

33
Under the Wall

The Sons of Gaia were too nervous to cross the harbor for fear of mines, so they trekked laboriously around its perimeter. Callum's feet grew sore after three days of scrambling through dense scrub. Finally, they reached a small, shaky bridge that spanned the narrowest neck of the harbor.

On the night they crossed the water, Quokka, Quoll, and Koala pitched camp under the shadow of the narrow bridge. Callum was sent to collect firewood. As he scouted in the brush, gathering up dry sticks, a wild-eyed stranger stepped out from behind a tree. His face was swollen and his eyes were bloodshot. He stretched one hand out to Callum, almost as if he were begging. Before Callum had time to react, the man let out a strangled cry and fell forward, a fishing spear in his back. A dark stain of blood spread across the ground.

Rusty came running through the brush, jumping over the man's body and putting his hands on Callum's shoulders. "Are you all right?" he asked.

"I'm fine. But you killed him. He may have only wanted help. He hadn't done anything and you killed him!"

"It doesn't matter what his intentions were, Callum. It is our responsibility to cull all strays."

Callum shut his eyes, remembering the kind, gentle man Rusty had been before he became a Son of Gaia.

Back at the campsite, Callum sat as far away from the men as he could while they ate a sloppy stew of ancient canned beans flavored with bitter herbs.

"You are very silent tonight, Fester," said Quoll, putting down his tin plate and staring at Callum.

"I'm tired," said Callum.

"If you had more faith in Gaia, she would sustain you," said Quoll. He turned to Rusty, frowning. "Koala, you said you educated the boy in the ways of Gaia. But still you call him by his name from your other life. If he is to serve us as we discussed, he must be reborn as a true Son of Gaia. You do not harbor feelings for him as a child of your flesh any longer, do you?"

Rusty blushed and put his head down. "No, brother, I harbor no feelings for him, other than brotherly love."

Callum glared at the top of his father's shiny bowed head.

"Then what will you name him?"

"We could call him Dibbler," said Rusty. "Dibblers were little desert animals, once native to the region where he grew up."

"Dibbler. A fine name for one destined to be a detonator."

"Dibbler the Detonator?" said Callum, trying to mask the ridicule in his voice.

A full moon rose over Vulture's Gate, and Callum lay awake for a long time, staring at the dappled light that shone through the gum trees. He flinched when Rusty came and lay beside him, and shut his eyes, pretending to be asleep. But when he opened them again, he realized Rusty was watching him, the way he had watched over him when he was small, his face full of tenderness.

"I wish we were all back in Nekhbet Tower," whispered Callum. "You, me, and Ruff. I wish you were tucking me into bed like when I was little."

"That time is over, Dibbler."

Callum winced. "I know that. I'm not a baby anymore. But it was a good time, wasn't it? We were happy then?"

Rusty's face grew still. He didn't answer.

"Do you know who Nekhbet was?" asked Rusty.

"It was just a name for the Tower, wasn't it?"

"No, it's not just a name. Nekhbet was a goddess of childbirth and motherhood. The Colony called the tower Nekhbet because they thought it was a good name for a nest of breeding humans. But 'Necropolis'—city of the dead—comes from the name of the sacred city in Egypt, Nekheb. The Colony coveted the name of a goddess of babies and death when they should have been looking to

Gaia. If we had embraced Gaia, then we would have understood our folly."

Callum wanted to cover his ears and scream. He turned his back on Rusty and willed himself into a dark and troubled sleep.

The next day they trekked along the edge of the harbor, into the heart of the ruined city. Rusty kept Callum close to him. Was it to keep him safe or to stop him escaping? Callum couldn't decide. He felt so numb with grief that all he could do was put one foot in front of the other.

When they came to the entrance to a flooded underground station, Callum wanted to laugh. It seemed like a lifetime ago that he and Bo had found their way into the Festers' cavern but the thought of her made him feel more alive. Quokka led the way down to the deepest part of the subway where he uncovered a canoe. They dragged it to the entrance of a watery tunnel that wound into blackness, deep under the city.

"Dibbler, Koala, you take the middle seat."

Callum could tell by the tone of Quokka's voice that he didn't trust either of them. He only wished that it were true—that Koala wasn't totally committed to the Sons of Gaia. As they glided through the dark caverns, the air grew chill and Callum began to shiver in the darkness. Finally, after what seemed like an eternity, they moored the canoe and climbed out onto a pile of broken rocks.

"Up through here," said Quokka, pointing to an opening through the rock face. "This is where the Sons have been working for the past year. We are so close to the surface, so close to infiltrating their stronghold, that explosives can't be used for fear of alerting Colony men. We believe there are fissures and small cracks that your beast may be able to detect that will provide us with the perfect location to lay our explosives. We will come with you until the space becomes too small. Then you must go forward alone to find the soft underbelly of the Wall."

They began to unload fuses and explosives from the canoe. Quoll strapped a huge coil of cable to Rusty's back, handed him two containers of explosives, and then pushed him toward the tunnel entrance.

As the passage narrowed, and began to wind upward, they were all reduced to crawling on their hands and knees, awkwardly maneuvering their equipment as they went. Finally they reached a small cave where another half-dozen containers of explosives were stored.

"This is as far as we have managed to dig effectively," said Quokka. "We need to find an open space directly beneath the Wall that we can fill with explosives. We believe it is only one hundred yards farther, but the route there may be circuitous."

Callum scrunched up his nose. The stale, close smell of the cave began to oppress him. He felt light-headed as he flicked open Mr. Pinkwhistle's chest and scrolled through to the screen that displayed the muon detector.

"Mr. Pinkwhistle's sensors show that there's one twisty tunnel that stretches for about a thousand feet but it's very narrow. Do you want him to go ahead?"

"No," said Quokka. "We want you to go. Follow the beast machine as far as is possible and establish fixed coordinates for your position. Then report back to us. The path to the location must be wide enough for you to drag the explosives with you, and the chosen position for the explosion must be large enough to store seven tins. Make note of the dimensions of the tunnels. When we are sure you have found a position directly beneath the Wall, we can begin in earnest."

While Quoll and Quokka sorted through the stockpile of tinned explosives, Rusty tied a loop of rope around Callum's waist.

"If anything goes wrong, if you run out of breath, or smell something that makes you giddy, tug three times and I'll haul you back to us," he said.

"Are you worried I'll run away?" asked Callum.

Rusty cupped Callum's face in his hands. "I trust you, Dibbler."

Callum wanted to shout, "Don't call me that! Don't trust me! I hate you. I wish it was you that died, not Ruff." But the heavy numbness that had descended on him since his reunion with Rusty squashed his rage deep inside.

He turned away and followed Mr. Pinkwhistle. The roboraptor sent out a soft blue light that filled the tunnel and made Callum less afraid. He was glad to be away from the men. When he was with Rusty he couldn't think straight, but alone with Mr. Pinkwhistle in the winding tunnels he remembered who he really was. And he remembered Bo, his dream of introducing her to his fathers and his hopes for their future. Now the future looked as dark as the narrow tunnel ahead of him.

It took Callum nearly twenty arduous minutes to reach

the cave that had shown up on Mr. Pinkwhistle's muon detector.

"We must be closer to the surface, Mr. P. The air smells better, doesn't it," he said, even though he knew there was no point in talking to the machine. Mr. Pinkwhistle bobbed his head and his eyes glowed pink as Callum checked his sensors and tried to figure out if they had come too far. Suddenly, Mr. Pinkwhistle jumped off Callum's lap and scurried ahead through the cavern.

"Mr. P, come back, come back," called Callum. He crawled on his belly to where the roboraptor had stopped at the bottom of a wide crevice. A thin shard of light pierced the darkness from above. Callum looked up to see a tunnel, almost like a chimney, that rose straight up through the rock. Halfway up, Callum could make out the beginnings of a ladder. Above the ladder, soft light filtered through a metal grid.

"I think we've come too far, Mr. P. I think we've passed under the Wall," said Callum.

The rope around Callum's waist grew tight, as someone yanked the other end. He tugged back, trying to loosen the knot but it was too hard to undo in the confined space. Wearily, he crawled back to the explosives stockpile. As he drew closer to the Sons of Gaia and the tunnel widened, he grabbed Mr. Pinkwhistle's tail and lay very still.

"Dibbler?" came Rusty's voice. "Are you there, Dibbler?"

Callum didn't answer. Tears filled his eyes. Why was he helping the Gaias? This man that called him Dibbler was nothing like Rusty. The old Rusty was lost to him. Next time the rope pulled tighter around his waist, he managed to undo the knot. It whisked its way down the tunnel and disappeared into the darkness.

"Callum! Callum!" shouted Rusty. "Callum, son, where are you?"

Callum started crawling again, drawn by the fear in his father's voice.

"It's all right, Dad," he said. "I'm coming."

As soon as Callum was near enough, Rusty dragged him into the open cave, into his arms. He held him so tightly Callum could hardly breathe. He ran his hands through Callum's hair and gazed into his face. For the first time since they'd discovered each other at the Gaias' aerie, Callum felt as if he could see his father again, the Rusty he had known and loved. He was glad that Quoll and Quokka were too far behind to see them or hear Rusty call him by his true name.

"I thought you'd drowned or were trapped. I thought I'd lost you again," whispered Rusty.

"I found the cave," said Callum. "There's plenty of room for the explosives, except I'll only be able to take one tin at a time through the passage. According to Mr. Pinkwhistle's muon detector, it should be directly under the Wall. We even went farther. I saw daylight! Daylight on the other side of the Wall!"

Rusty ran his hand over Callum's face, like a blind man. "I don't want you to do this, Callum," he said, his voice breaking. "I don't want you to be the detonator."

"It's okay," said Callum. "Maybe if the Wall comes

down, I'll be able to get out to the island and see Bo again. If I could only see her one more time . . ."

"Callum, you haven't understood," interrupted Rusty. "When Quoll and Quokka said we're to be the detonators, they mean we will detonate the bombs. You'll die in the blast. I was going to use you to help me trigger the explosives."

Callum looked into Rusty's eyes and saw the truth.

"Detonators for Gaia," he said. "You were going to kill me?"

"We were going to die together. But I don't want you to do it, Callum. I want you to live."

Callum pressed his face against Rusty's chest. It was the old Rusty again but it was too late. There was too little time left.

"What can we do? They'll kill us both anyway."

Rusty's hands were trembling as he tied the rope around Callum's waist again. "No," said Rusty. "You are going to live."

34
The *Bouboulina*

Callum pushed Mr. Pinkwhistle through the opening in the gutter and wrapped his fingers around the bars of the storm water grate. As another explosion reverberated through the tunnel, a backwash of water flooded the drain and dragged him off his feet. He clung to the metal bars with all his strength while Mr. Pinkwhistle crouched above him, mewling in distress.

"Shut up, Mr. P," he said. When the worst of the shockwaves had subsided he pushed the grate aside and dragged himself into the gutter. The streetlights were out and the fires along the Wall cast a smoky orange glow across the roadway. Squadrones and Colony men raced down the streets, heading for the Wall, frantic to battle the invisible enemy. Callum clutched Mr. Pinkwhistle against his chest and ran in the opposite direction. Tumbling over a low fence, he lay flat on his belly, listening to the sound of the Colony alarms screaming.

The night air felt cool against his burning face but his ears were still ringing from the roar of the explosion. He couldn't believe he was alive. He shut his eyes and tried to recall those last moments beneath the Wall with his father. "Yesterday was mine," Rusty had said. "I messed it up. But all the tomorrows are for you, Callum. However few of them are left. You are the future. Take it and run with it." Then he'd hugged Callum tightly and kissed him one last time before pushing him into the narrow tunnels that led to freedom.

But freedom was like drowning. Callum had no idea what to do next. He had nowhere to go, no one to turn to. Except Bo. Moving quickly and quietly and keeping low to the ground, Callum made his way to the waterfront. If he could find any small vessel that would take him across the harbor to the Island, he would risk the mines. He would risk anything to be with Bo again.

He forced his way through a maze of barbed wire and scrambled along the rocky edge of the harbor in the dark. Jagged stones cut his feet and he stumbled on mounds of slippery seaweed as he made his way along the shore. He had almost given up hope of finding a vessel when he heard strange voices drifting down to the water from somewhere above.

The shrieks and cries were emanating from a golden terrace, where a crowd of children were clustered, watching the collapse of the South Wall. Callum stopped and stared, transfixed. They weren't ordinary boys. They were dressed in colorful flowing costumes, the kind he'd only seen in picture books of the olden times. The kind that only girls had worn.

Callum flung himself at the harbor wall and clambered upward, forcing his way through more layers of barbed wire. He hid at the bottom of the garden, studying the figures of the girls on the terrace. One girl stood near the railing, dressed in a long turquoise outfit. Something in her stance sent a shiver of recognition through Callum. He put Mr. Pinkwhistle down on the smooth green lawn. "Find her, Mr. Pinkwhistle. If she's up there, find Bo."

Bo watched as another explosion made the whole of South Head shudder. The girls of the Zenana ran about the terrace in a frenzy of excitement and distress. Serene began to scream again, pushing her hands against her pink cheeks, her mouth a perfect circle of horror. Several of the smaller girls joined in while Meera and Verity hurried from one child to the next, trying to comfort them and herd them back inside. Lolly ran to Bo, her face full of fear, begging to be picked up.

"Who could have done that?" asked Li-Li, watching the plumes of black smoke and debris.

Bo stood at the cast-iron railing with Lolly on her hip. "Perhaps it's Festers, perhaps they've come to destroy the Colony at last."

"Then they've sent something strange in their advance guard," said Li-Li. She pointed at a small creature charging out of the shrubbery. "What is that?"

Bo stared in disbelief, her heart in her mouth.

Mr. Pinkwhistle was scurrying across the lawn, making a beeline for the terrace. She put Lolly down and pulled Mr. Pinkwhistle over the railing, holding his chipped and battered body to her chest.

"Someone has come for me," she said.

Li-Li gripped her arm. "The Festers? The Festers have come for us? Are there many of them? Have they come to take us all?"

Bo bent over the terrace railing and scanned the grounds. "I don't know. But there is one boy who must be out there, one boy at least. And I have to find him." She couldn't bear to say his name, in case it wasn't true.

"Take me with you," said Li-Li, gripping Bo's hand.

"I don't know where I'm going, Li-Li. It may not be safe."

"Nothing's safe. Wherever you're going, I want to come."

"I want to come, too," said Lolly, clinging to Bo's knees.

Bo knelt beside Lolly and hugged her tightly, breathing in the sweet scent of her body, stroking her long curls. "You'll be safe here," said Bo.

"No she won't," said Li-Li softly.

They both looked back into the chaotic living room where Verity and Meera were trying to calm the smaller girls. "Not one of them is safe here, Bo," said Li-Li. "They'll all end up on Mater Misericordiae."

Bo felt as if the weight of the world had settled on her shoulders. She cupped Lolly's face in her hands and stared into her eyes. "I want you to go back inside, Lolly."

"But I want to come," said Lolly, her bottom lip quivering.

"Then you be good and wait for me. I promise I'll come for you," said Bo.

"How can you promise that?" asked Li-Li.

"How can I not promise?" said Bo grimly.

Once Lolly was back in the house, Bo scanned the gardens. Nothing moved.

"He's out there somewhere," she said, as much to herself as to Li-Li. "He's out there waiting for me."

Bo tore the skirt from her dress and then turned to Li-Li and ripped away the folds of fabric from the other girl's costume, shredding the cloth and knotting it to form a makeshift rope. "Are you ready?"

Li-Li smiled and tied the end of the cloth around the railing. "I go where you go," she said.

Bo felt beads of sweat trickle down her forehead as she lowered Li-Li into the garden.

As soon as Li-Li hit the ground, Callum ran toward the terrace wall, stopping in surprise when Li-Li turned and smiled at him.

"You've come to save us, haven't you?"

"I've come for Bo," Callum replied.

At that moment, Bo landed beside them. She grabbed Callum in an awkward embrace, squashing Mr. Pinkwhistle between them. "Where are the rest of the Festers?"

"There's no one else—only me. Aren't I enough?" said Callum, unable to wipe the grin from his face.

Bo laughed. "You are everyone and everything that matters. And you are crazy." She ran her hand over the top of his head, feeling the roughness of his short hair. "But now what? Should we search for your fathers? Maybe they're somewhere in the Colony. Then they can help us, the way you always said they would."

Callum's face grew dark. "They can't help." He hung his head and stuttered as he spoke. "Ruff is dead. He died before we even reached Vulture's Gate. And Rusty's gone, too. He was under the Wall with me. We loaded up a cave full of explosives that I was meant to detonate. But then he made me get out. He did it alone. He sent me ahead and waited. He died for me, he died so I could live."

Callum's voice cracked as he spoke. "I had to see you, Bo. I had to see you one more time before we both die, too."

Bo pulled him toward her and held him close. "It's all right now. We're together again."

"You two are so sloppy," said Li-Li. "You may be ready to die. But I'm not."

Bo stepped away from Callum. "Then we have to get off South Head."

"We can escape by sea," said Li-Li, turning to Bo. "Hackett has a ship. He keeps it moored at the dock near the Zenana."

"But the harbor is full of mines," said Callum.

"I know," said Li-Li. "But the *Bouboulina* is a minesweeper. She's indestructible. She's made of glass-reinforced plastic and she has a set of ROVs, little robotic boats that they send ahead to blow the mines. You can see her from the end of the garden."

Bo and Callum followed Li-Li to where the Zenana

was separated from the harbor by a high barbed-wire fence. Callum stared dubiously at the gray minesweeper moored at the pier. Even Bo felt a flicker of uncertainty as she looked at the *Bouboulina*, heavy and forbidding in the approaching twilight. Behind it the harbor glowed blood red and orange as the sun set behind the smoking city, an apocalyptic vision of hell.

"I don't know how to use all the sonar and radar," said Li-Li. "But I do know how to sail her. I was born on a boat. My mother's family were all sea people. And I've been out on the *Bouboulina* before. With Hackett," said Li-Li. She looked down at her bare legs and blushed.

Callum frowned and looked from Li-Li to Bo. "I was thinking more of a little boat," he said. "One that three people can manage. I don't see how we can get away on that thing."

"Callum, there's something I wanted to tell you about," said Bo. "We are more than three . . ."

"Yes, we can't leave the others," said Li-Li.

"What others?" asked Callum.

"The other girls in the Zenana. They don't deserve what will happen to them. Hackett and the Colony men, they'll hurt them the way they hurt me. Then they'll take them out to the Island to die."

"We can't save everyone," said Callum. His face looked tired and drawn, as if in the weeks since Bo had last seen him he had aged years.

"Yes we can," said Li-Li "The *Bouboulina* can take thirty. There are only seventeen other girls at the Zenana."

"Seventeen!" said Callum.

35
Flight

The gardens of the Zenana were eerily quiet as Bo, Callum, and Li-Li crept back up to the house. Inside the lounge room, Meera and Verity had managed to settle the girls, forcing them to sit on the floor in three rows, their hands folded in their laps.

"Wait here," said Bo, stationing Callum and Mr. Pinkwhistle beside the terrace doors.

"But what are you going to do? They're big women. They look like men. You can't overpower them."

"No," said Li-Li, "but if Bo follows my cues, we'll have all the girls outside within the hour."

As soon as Bo and Li-Li stepped over the threshold, chaos threatened to break out again in the living room. All the girls began talking at once. Lolly pushed her way past Meera and Verity and threw herself at Bo.

"Not now, Lolly," said Bo, ready to fight. But Lolly wrapped herself around one of Bo's legs while Verity grabbed hold of Bo's arm and dragged her down the steps. At the same time, Meera gripped Li-Li by her hair and pulled her across the room. But Li-Li didn't resist. "Where have you been?" shouted Meera. "What's happened to your dress?"

"There are hundreds of Festers and strange men outside! They tore our skirts off!" said Li-Li. Bo looked across at her in surprise. It hadn't occurred to her that lying would save them but Verity and Meera instantly released both girls and ran to lock the doors and draw the curtains.

"Squadrones are on their way to defend us," said Meera. "As soon as they are here, all the girls will be taken out to the island. The Pally-vals will arrive any moment. We must stay calm."

Li-Li picked up Ritisha, one of the smallest girls beside Lolly, and held her in her arms. Bo wondered what she was planning and a minute later she understood. Ritisha began to wail and writhe, hitting out at Li-Li with all the strength her plump little body could muster.

"I'm sorry, Lolly," said Bo, sweeping the toddler into her arms and then pinching her so hard that Lolly, too, began to howl. "Good girl," whispered Bo. "Be loud. Be very loud."

"What are you doing! Settle those two down, now!" commanded Meera.

"She's hysterical," shouted Li-Li. "It's not my fault. And she's set off Lolly, too. Should we put them in the Black Boxes until the Squadrones arrive?"

Bo suddenly understood what Li-Li was planning. Only Meera and Verity carried the keys to the punishment rooms. When they reached the top of the stairs and Meera opened the door to the first tiny soundproof room, Bo and Li-Li acted in concert to push her inside and slam the door shut. Five minutes later they had Verity locked in the second room.

As they walked back downstairs, Bo kissed Lolly on the cheek and stroked the pink mark on her leg where she'd pinched her. "You were very brave. I'm sorry I had to hurt you but I needed your help."

"Helping hurts," said Lolly, putting her thumb in her mouth.

"Yes," said Bo. "Sometimes being helpful hurts but it's a very good thing to do."

In the living room, all the girls were talking at once. Li-Li stood on a chair and shouted for their attention.

"There are no Festers outside," she announced. "That was a lie. But there is one boy out there who is Bo's friend. A clever boy, not a stupid boy. He's like . . . the soldier in the story of *The Twelve Dancing Princesses*. So I don't want any of you to be afraid of him or to treat him badly."

"But what is he doing here?" asked Serene.

"He's come to rescue us. If we let Meera and Verity take us to the Island, cruel men will hurt us. Bo and I are the only girls who have been to the Island and come back, and we can tell you it is a bad, bad place. So we're all running away. Together. Right now."

She jumped down from the chair and grabbed Serene

with one hand and the sniveling Ritisha with the other. "That should do it," she said, as an aside to Bo.

Callum looked bewildered as the girls poured out of the Zenana and surrounded him, their faces full of curiosity and admiration.

"You've come to rescue us," said Serene, smiling up at Callum.

"I guess so," he said.

They streamed down through the garden, their skirts and veils flowing out behind them. Li-Li led the way and Mr. Pinkwhistle ran alongside, as if he were shepherding them toward the fence.

"This is like a very strange dream," said Callum.

"Pray that when we wake up, we'll be far away from here," said Bo.

When they reached the water's edge, Bo set Mr. Pinkwhistle to work, using his titanium jaws to snap through the tangle of barbed wire that lay in great curling piles all along the waterfront. Once the roboraptor had cleared the way, they pushed through to the water, scrambling over semisubmerged rocks to the dock of the *Bouboulina*. Callum, Li-Li, and Bo lifted the smaller girls onto the wharf one by one. Bo was the last to climb up onto the weathered timber. A premonition of disaster washed over her. It almost felt too easy as they walked along the dark and deserted pier toward the minesweeper. She glanced up at the side of the boat at the same moment as a small, pale face appeared at the rail.

Before she could stop him, Callum had cried out. "Flakie! It's us, Callum and Bo. Flakie, let down the ramp."

He raised one arm to wave. Li-Li tried to stop him but it was too late. Flakie bent over the rail clutching a gun in both hands, and fired. Callum fell forward, one hand pressed against the bloody wound to his shoulder, his face blank with shock. Bo knelt beside him, his head in her lap as the girls crowded around him. She pulled his hand away from the wound and blood gushed from his shoulder.

"No, this can't be happening!" she said, as she pushed her hand against the wound to stem the flow of blood.

"Why did he do that?" asked Callum, gasping in pain. "It was Flakie."

"He's a drone," said Li-Li. "They do what they're instructed to do."

"You should run," said Callum. "Leave me and hide."

Li-Li snorted with exasperation. "We're girls. He can't hurt us. Only boys. And if he's the only one on board, he won't be hard to get rid of."

"It will be all right," said Bo, putting her cheek against Callum's. "Everything will be all right."

"We must go now," said Li-Li.

"I can't leave him."

"If you want to save him, you'll do as I say. I need your help. We have to climb the ship's anchor to get on board. Then we can come back for him. The girls will take care of him. As long as they shelter him with their bodies, Flakie won't fire again. He won't risk hurting one of us."

The little girls closed in around Callum, making a circle of protection over his body, and Bo stepped away.

"Mr. Pinkwhistle will guard you, too," she said. "I'll come back for you, I promise."

Callum didn't answer. His eyes were shut and his face was stiff with pain.

Bo followed Li-Li to where the minesweeper's anchor chain stretched into the water. Li-Li leaped from the dock onto the long chain and scrambled up toward the deck like a monkey. Bo did the same.

Once on board, they headed straight to the cabin on the forecastle. As they turned a corner, they came face-to-face with Flakie. He was still carrying his weapon but he stared at them as vacantly as if he were holding a teatray.

Li-Li held Bo back. "Watch this," she said. She grabbed Flakie by the front of his uniform, snatched the gun from his hands, and dragged him over to the edge of the deck where there was only a section of chain as a railing. Without letting go of him, she undid the chain and then leaned her face close to his—so close that it looked as if she were about to kiss him. Flakie teetered on the brink trying to avoid her lips, flailing for something to grasp other than Li-Li. Then he fell, mutely, into the dark harbor water.

Li-Li laughed and hurried back to Bo's side. "The boys they've trained for the Zenana won't touch you, no matter what. And they'll do anything to escape being kissed. If your face gets too close, they panic. They're morons. We used to make them fall in the pool all the time. It was such fun. As soon as they dragged themselves out, we'd do it again."

Bo leaned over the railing, scanning the water for Flakie. She breathed a sigh of relief when she saw him scrambling up the side of the dock. At least he hadn't drowned.

Li-Li slipped her hand into Bo's and led her to the bottom of a small flight of stairs that led to the forecastle. At the top of the stairs, a sliver of light shone out from beneath a door. It opened, and as the light flooded down the stairwell the shadow of a man fell across their upturned faces.

"Two foundlings," said Hackett. "How charming. I always said Misericordiae-brewed girls might be better breeders, but you foundlings are much more fun."

"Hackett," said Li-Li. "I'm so glad to see you."

She raised the gun that she'd taken from Flakie and fired a single shot into his chest. For a split second, Hackett looked surprised before he fell forward, tumbling down the stairs to lie in a heap at their feet.

"What have you done, Li-Li?" said Bo, kneeling beside the body.

"I hope I've killed him," she replied. "He deserved it for what he did to me. And what he would have done to you, and the other girls, if he'd had the chance."

Bo looked up at Li-Li as if seeing her for the first time. Li-Li gripped the pistol, her knuckles white. Gently, Bo pushed Li-Li's hands down, forcing her to lower the gun.

"We have to bring the others on board. You lower the ramp, and I'll check the boat for other men."

Bo was relieved to find the cabins below deck were all empty. As soon as she'd finished her task, she ran down the ramp and onto the dock. The girls stepped aside and she fell to her knees beside Callum. He lay like a broken doll, his head at an odd angle, his body limp. She picked him up carefully, cradling his head against her chest. Warm blood seeped from his shoulder, soaking into the bodice of her torn and dirty dress.

Li-Li called to them as the girls ran up the ramp and boarded the *Bouboulina*. Mr. Pinkwhistle let out a low, guttural growl and his eyes glowed a brighter red.

"No, Mr. Pinkwhistle, follow," said Bo. But the roboraptor went skittering down the pier to where two squadrons were clumping onto the dock. Bo heard the men roar in surprise as the roboraptor attacked their legs. Struggling under Callum's weight, she staggered up the ramp. She laid him tenderly on a bunk in one of the cabins and covered him with a blanket.

"I won't be long. I'll come back to you soon," she said.

When Bo climbed on deck, all the girls were clustered at the railing watching the ramp retract and squealing at something that was happening below. Down on the dock, Mr. Pinkwhistle was slashing the Squadrones' legs with his teeth. They tried to smash him with their gun butts but he was too nimble for them. He wove his way between their legs, snapping with such speed that the drones jumped to one side to avoid him, as if they were all caught up in a crazy dance. Bo put her fingers between her teeth and let out a long, shrill whistle. In an instant, Mr. Pinkwhistle had raced to the end of the dock and launched himself into the air, landing neatly on the deck beside Bo. She picked him up and hurried to the forecastle.

"They're coming for us," she told Li-Li. "Can you really do this? Can you get us out?"

Li-Li kissed her lightly on the cheek and turned to the minesweeper's controls. The *Bouboulina* surged away from the dock.

"Go and take care of your boy," said Li-Li.

36
Once Upon a Time

As Bo descended the stairs from the forecastle, the first harbor mine exploded and sent a shudder through the bow of the boat. She reached to steady herself and realized something was wrong. Hackett. He wasn't lying at the bottom of the stairs anymore. A dark stain of blood on the floor marked where he had been.

Outside, the first rays of dawn light were creeping across the water. Bo scanned the main deck anxiously. There was no sign of Hackett. Surely he couldn't have escaped?

The *Bouboulina* surged into the harbor, leaving a trail of white water in its wake. The girls stood at the rails, watching the shoreline and the Zenana receding from view. Against a lightening sky, columns of smoke billowed above the Colony. All along South Head, red-tiled roofs were collapsing. Rocked by explosions, the Wall continued to topple into a pile of rubble. Bo crossed the deck to join Lolly, who was clutching the railing, the wind blowing her curls out behind her. At the sound of Bo's footsteps Lolly turned, but the beginnings of her smile were replaced by a scream. Something clipped Bo hard across the back of the head.

"Where's the other little slut?" asked Hackett, his voice slurred with pain. Bo didn't answer. Despite her throbbing head, she leaped at him, knocking him over with the force of her attack. She aimed a blow to his face but Hackett grabbed her arm and twisted it hard before she made contact. She let out an involuntary cry of pain, then sank her teeth into his wrist until she could taste his salty blood and he roared in wounded rage. Suddenly Hackett was on top of her, his huge hands around her throat, squeezing the breath from her body. As if from faraway, she could hear the small girls screaming and, above the commotion, someone shouting. Hackett released Bo and turned to face Li-Li.

"Where did you think you could run to?" sneered Hackett. "There's nothing out there for you. For you or your little girlfriends."

Li-Li glared at him and pointed the gun at his chest but Bo could see that she was trembling. It would be harder to pull the trigger a second time.

Hackett took a step closer.

"You were safe in the Colony, Li-Li."

"I don't want to be safe, if safety is what you gave me," said Li-Li. "I want to be free."

Hackett laughed and a little fleck of blood flew from his mouth and landed on Li-Li's cheek. Even though his chest was sticky with blood, he stepped toward her and reached for the gun.

"Girls like you will never be free in this world," said Hackett.

Suddenly, as if from nowhere, Callum appeared, swinging a pole with all the force left in his wounded body. He brought it down hard across Hackett's arm. Then he stepped in closer, wielding the pole like a club, beating Hackett around the head and shoulders. Man and boy careered across the deck, crashing into the railing. Hackett grabbed the end of the pole and wrenched it from Callum. Callum slumped, as if the pole were the only thing that had given him strength. For a split second, Bo thought Hackett would fling Callum from the ship. In the same instant, Li-Li and Bo ran to Callum's aid and with a mighty push, they forced Hackett over the railing and into the harbor. His pale face bobbed up and down in the water, washed with the first morning light.

"Oh no," said Li-Li. "Look."

Speeding toward Hackett, their decks crowded with Squadrones, was a flotilla of small speedboats, safe in the wake of the *Bouboulina* and the mine-free path it had cleared through the harbor.

The first speedboat slowed to haul Hackett on board and was quickly overtaken by the rest of the flotilla. There were six of them, racing toward the slow-moving minesweeper. Any minute they would come alongside and board the *Bouboulina*.

"They'll take us back to the Zenana," said Serene, stepping up to the railing. "They'll take us back and this time they'll really punish us," she sobbed.

The girls crowded together in the bow of the boat, watching the speedboats draw closer. "I'd rather die than go back," said Li-Li.

"No one's going to die," said Bo. She put two fingers between her teeth and whistled loudly. Mr. Pinkwhistle scurried between the legs of the girls, searching for Bo, then jumped into her arms. "Stand back," said Bo. "Keep away from the edge, big girls help the little ones and brace yourself for rough seas."

Bo opened Mr. Pinkwhistle's chest and began to make calculations. When he was primed, she positioned him carefully on the deck with his head tilted upward. Then she ran to join Callum where he sat slumped against a pile of ropes and canvas.

"What is he going to do?" asked Callum.

"Something I've never made him do before," said Bo. She put her arms around Callum and braced them both for the shockwaves.

Mr. Pinkwhistle's jaw flipped open, so wide it almost looked as though it was dislocated. A gargling sound came out of his body and then suddenly, a tiny missile launched out of his mouth, shooting over the stern of the boat, directly into the path of the speedboats. One after another, miniature missiles released in lightning succession from Mr. Pinkwhistle's open jaw. Sparks and smoke spilled from him as his body was racked by each release. A plume of seawater fifty feet high rose into the air, showering the deck.

The girls shrieked as they were drenched with cold water but when the turbulence had settled, they ran to the railing. The flotilla was in disarray. Four speedboats had capsized and the others had stopped to haul men from the water.

Mr. Pinkwhistle snapped his jaw shut and spun in a circle three times, a dance of victory, while the girls gathered around him and cheered.

When they were sure they were safe, the children all climbed the stairs to the upper deck and crowded onto the forecastle. Bo helped Callum into a seat beside Li-Li and checked his wound. It had stopped bleeding. The bullet hadn't lodged in his shoulder but had cut through the outer edge, leaving a deep flesh wound that would heal with time.

Wearily, Callum pushed her hands away. "Stop fussing. I'm all right," he said. "I'm more worried about what happens next. They'll hunt us down, you know, no matter where we go in the harbor. Even if we hide on the North Shore, there will be Sons of Gaia waiting to poison us. There's nowhere safe in Vulture's Gate."

"I know," said Li-Li. "That's why we're leaving. We're not sailing across the harbor. I've sent the ROVs ahead to clear the mines all along the peninsula. We're going to sail through the Heads."

"Into the open sea?" said Callum. "But where do we go from there?"

"To find a home," said Bo. "Our own home in a faraway place."

"That sounds like one of your stories. What if there is nowhere safe? What if there's nothing out there?"

"Before I met you, I thought all boys were idiots," said Li-Li. "Don't prove me right."

Callum smiled. "Before Bo, I thought all girls were extinct. I'm ready to be wrong again."

Bo glanced from Callum to Li-Li and laughed. Then she looked out to the wide, open sea, to the vast, deep blue expanse of ocean lying between the golden cliffs. In a matter of minutes, they would pass out of the harbor. Vulture's Gate would be left behind. She wanted to feel happy and free at last but there was a part of her that felt heavy with loss. All her old life was gone forever. Poppy, Tjukurpa Piti, the Daisy-May, Mollie Green, Roc and the Festers, even her time at the Zenana were over forever. Every moment of those other lives that she had lived was now only a story. She glanced from Li-Li to Callum. She wasn't alone. Each of them had lost so much. The weary faces of all the Colony girls were etched with hope and nervous anticipation. The future was an open book.

"Will our story have a good ending?" asked Serene.

"Yes," said Li-Li firmly. "We'll find an island. But not like Mater Misericordiae. A new island where girls can be free."

"And they all lived happily ever after," said Lolly, looking up at the older children.

"But that's what you say at the end of the story," said Bo, sweeping Lolly into her arms. "This isn't the end."

"What goes at the start?"

"Once upon a time . . ."